M000098544

THE ADVENTURES OF
LAZARUS GRAY
VOLUME ELEVEN
THIRTY PIECES OF SILVER

BY BARRY REESE

Also available by Barry Reese from REESE UNLIMITED and published by Pro Se Press:

The Peregrine Omnibus - Volumes 1-3
The Adventures of Lazarus Gray
The Adventures of Gravedigger

Other Works
The Family Grace: An Extraordinary History
Rabbit Heart
The Damned Thing
The Second Book of Babylon
Assistance Unlimited: The Silver Age – Broken Empire
Worlds Apart

THE ADVENTURES OF LAZARUS GRAY, VOLUME ELEVEN

A Reese Unlimited Book
Published by Pro Se Press

"Secrets of the Dead" Copyright © 2014 - 2022 Barry Reese & George Sellas
"Thirty Pieces of Silver", and "Timeline" Copyright © 2022, Barry Reese

Cover By Jeffrey Hayes
Interior Illustration by George Sellas
Print Production and Book Design by Sean E. Ali
E-Book Design by Antonio lo Iacono and Marzia Marina

New Pulp Seal created by Cari Reese

The stories in this publication are fictional. All of the characters in this publication are fictitious and any resemblance to actual persons, living or dead is purely coincidental. No part of this publication may be reproduced or transmitted in any form or by any means, graphic, electronic, or mechanical, including photocopying, recording, taping or by any information storage or retrieval system, without the permission in writing of the publisher.

Edited by Dale Russell
Editor in Chief, Pro Se Productions-Tommy Hancock
Publisher and Pro Se Productions, LLC-Chief Executive Officer-Fuller Bumpers

Pro Se Productions, LLC
133 1/2 Broad Street
Batesville, AR, 72501
870-834-4022

editorinchief@prose-press.com
www.prose-press.com

The Adventures of Lazarus Gray, Volume Eleven
Copyright © 2022 Pro Se Productions
All rights reserved.

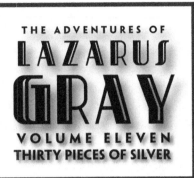

THE ADVENTURES OF

LAZARUS GRAY

VOLUME ELEVEN
THIRTY PIECES OF SILVER

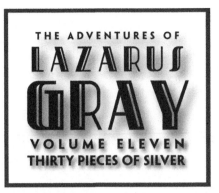

THE ADVENTURES OF
LAZARUS GRAY
VOLUME ELEVEN
THIRTY PIECES OF SILVER

TABLE OF CONTENTS

THE SOVEREIGN
CITY PROJECT ™

SECRETS OF THE DEAD
THE ORIGIN OF LAZARUS GRAY

LAZARUS GRAY

IN SECRETS OF THE DEAD

BY BARRY REESE & GEORGE SELLAS

ASSISTANCE UNLIMITED
6196 ROBESON AVENUE

BORN TO WEALTHY SAN FRANCISCO PARENTS, RICHARD WINTHROP ATTENDED YALE UNIVERSITY AND GRADUATED WITH HONORS.

BUT ON THE DAY OF HIS GRADUATION, HE WAS APPROACHED BY WALTHER LUNT, WHO OFFERED HIM A PLACE WITHIN THE SHADOWY ORGANIZATION KNOWN AS **THE ILLUMINATI.**

HIS NATURAL INTEREST IN THE SUPERNATURAL SUDDENLY UNLEASHED, RICHARD ACCOMPANIED LUNT AROUND THE WORLD, INVESTIGATING THE UNKNOWN.

ALONG THE WAY, HE MET MIYA SHIMADA, A LOVELY JAPANESE-AMERICAN WHO WON HIS HEART.

BUT EVENTUALLY WINTHROP LEARNED THE TRUTH ABOUT THE ILLUMINATI AND THE VILE SECRETS THAT THEY POSSESSED. REBELLING, HE BECAME AN ENEMY TO THE MEN AND WOMEN HE HAD ONCE TRUSTED.

SHOT AND LEFT FOR DEAD ON THE SHORES OF SOVEREIGN CITY, RICHARD WINTHROP HAD NO MEMORY OF WHO OR WHAT HE WAS. THE ONLY CLUE TO HIS IDENTITY WAS A SMALL MEDALLION WITH THE WORDS 'LAZARUS GRAY' STAMPED UPON IT.

UNAWARE THAT LAZARUS GRAY HAD BEEN THE FALSE IDENTITY OF THE ILLUMINATI'S FOUNDER, WINTHROP TOOK THE NAME AS HIS OWN, IN THE HOPES THAT IT WOULD DRAW OUT THOSE WHO KNEW THE TRUTH ABOUT HIS PAST.

RESURRECTED AS A HERO, LAZARUS GRAY NOW FIGHTS TO MAKE UP FOR THE EVIL ACTS HE TOOK PART IN WITH THE ILLUMINATI. AIDED BY OTHERS WHO HAVE SIMILAR PASTS, LAZARUS GRAY HELPS MAKE SURE THAT THE INNOCENTS OF SOVEREIGN CITY CAN SLEEP PEACEFULLY IN THEIR BEDS!

THIRTY PIECES OF SILVER
AN ADVENTURE STARRING LAZARUS GRAY

"Thirty pieces of silver"

Burns on the traitor's brain;

"Thirty pieces of silver!

Oh! It is hellish gain!"

—*Thirty Pieces of Silver* by William Blane

CHAPTER I
FIELD OF BLOOD

36 A.D.

THE RAIN FELL steadily, soaking him to the bone. His clothes were plastered to his pale skin and he had to keep blinking as the drops collected in his long lashes, obscuring his vision. Though he'd spent the money he'd been given for his awful deed, he imagined that he could still feel the weight of the coins in his pockets…weighing him down like an anchor upon his soul.

He took several staggering steps towards a large tree. It was silhouetted against the gray sky, a single length of rope in the shape of a noose hanging down from one of the branches. He'd tied it earlier, testing its length and strength, but he thought he'd be using it before the storm came…he'd been wrong as the thunder and dark clouds had rolled in earlier than expected.

His sandaled feet sank deep into the mud, making a squelching sound every time he lifted his leg for another step. Akeldama was the local name given to this field and he'd purchased it two days before, wanting to rid himself of the cursed money as soon as possible. Unfortunately, tales of his treachery had reached the land's owners and they refused to take the accursed coins…he was forced to buy it with other monies. In the end, he'd buried the thirty pieces of silver in the very center of this field—before the rains came, he had been able to spot the displaced earth where he'd dug a small hole with a knife and shoved the coins in before covering it over with dirt. Now the location was lost in a sea of mud—but he felt confident that the coins would not wash back up. They were quite deep.

Reaching the tree, he began to climb. He moved slowly, not wanting to slip and fall…and then the absurdity of his situation caused him to throw back his head and laugh. Why move so carefully when he was planning to kill himself?

Inching along the limb, he seized hold of the wet rope and pulled the noose around his neck. He adjusted it until it was quite snug against his skin and he felt a tingling in his lips—it reminded him of kissing Jesus on the cheek, an act which was not meant to be a sign of devotion or respect. It was a sign to the watching guards that this was the man they sought—for thirty pieces of silver, Judas Iscariot had betrayed Christ. Because of him, Jesus had been crucified and Judas' soul was forever damned.

Taking one last breath, the traitor to God's only son flung himself from the tree limb. He felt a tightening about his neck, uncomfortably cutting off his airflow, and his legs began to kick. He realized that he had misjudged the necessary length of rope…at the appropriate length it would have broken his neck immediately…but if it was too long, as this undoubtedly was, then he was in for a painful demise.

Despite his desire for death, his body had other ideas and his fingers came up to try and pull the rope away. He was unable to loosen the bonds that were now digging into his flesh and his face began to change colors as he twisted and turned. Through the tears that began to sting his eyes, he saw a half dozen figures walking into the field, each wearing hooded robes of the brightest scarlet. The robes were so all-encompassing that Judas was unable to tell the gender or ethnicity of the wearers.

For a moment he thought they would rush forward and save him— but even as he thrashed about, he realized that they would not. They did move towards him but they stopped about half way and Judas watched with wide eyes as two of the robed figures knelt and began digging in the mud.

"No," he tried to hiss but no sound came out—and even if it had, it would have been swallowed up by the rolling thunder that crashed overhead.

One of the hooded strangers rose, clutching the satchel tightly in one hand. Within the bag lay the cursed silver coins, tainted forever by Judas' sin.

"No," Judas tried to repeat…and then all went dark, forever.

—⊂⧉⊃—

August 1942

He strode into the room like a king, despite the fact he looked ludicrous in his green-and-yellow checkered attire. The Puzzler's real name was not known to any of his gang—as far as they knew, or cared, he had sprung full-blown into existence as the master gamesman that the press had dubbed *The Puzzle-Master of Crime!*

The Puzzler grinned at the well-polished Germans that rose to greet him. These men amused him—they snuck into the country and pretended to be Americans but the first chance they got, they were decked out in their Nazi uniforms.

Captain Albrecht Krieger clicked his heels together and delivered a crisp "Heil Hitler" salute. Krieger was the epitome of the Aryan ideal, with close-cropped blond hair, piercing blue eyes, and an athletic build. When he saw that The Puzzler did not return the salute, Krieger's expression darkened. "Herr Puzzler, did you manage to retrieve the item?"

"Of course I did," The Puzzler replied, moving past the German Captain and plopping down in the chair that Krieger had occupied only seconds before. "I'm the best when it comes to solving mental puzzles, aren't I? And a security system is nothing but a little test, just waiting to be bested by someone with the right intelligence level."

Krieger thrust a black-gloved hand towards the American criminal. "Then give it to me."

A wry grin appeared on The Puzzler's lips and he leaned back in the chair, regarding the German with an expression of contempt. "Not so fast, Nazi. I know that you and your Fuehrer want this little trinket really badly...maybe a little more badly than what you've already paid me?"

"You're asking for more money?" Krieger asked, a twitch appeared on his forehead. "You Americans are so motivated by greed. Have you no honor?"

"Don't talk to me about honor, Nazi," The Puzzler spat. "I have a cousin that's German. A German *Jew*. I know what you people are doing over there."

"You have Jewish blood in you? I cannot say that I'm surprised." Krieger noticeably placed a hand atop his holstered gun, not-so-casually unbuttoning the leather strap that held it in place. "I do not believe in renegotiating...though I know it's in your blood to try and cheat your business partners."

The Puzzler rose from his seat, standing so close to Krieger that the two men were practically nose-to-nose. "I don't want any more of your Fuehrer's blood money, Captain. I want my cousin. I want him freed from that damned camp you threw him into and I want him brought here to America. Give me that in writing and then I'll give you your prize."

Krieger stared into the American's eyes for a long moment. He saw madness, yes, but also a steely resolve: this strangely-garbed man meant what he said... Krieger considered simply killing the man and taking what he wanted but there was always the chance that The Puzzler had considered that possibility and hidden the object that the Fuehrer sought. "Very well, Herr Puzzler," Krieger said at length. The German Captain raised one hand and gestured to one of his men, who produced a pen and paper from the interior of his jacket. Krieger took these and waited for the man to turn about, offering his back for his captain to press down upon. "I will write this in English for you, my friend...but you must realize that I will have to get this cleared by my superiors in Berlin."

"That's fine. I'll just hold on to the prize until I get my cousin."

"That's not what we agreed upon," Krieger said, freezing in place. "You said if I gave you this in writing..."

"No need to repeat it. I was here." The Puzzler grinned once more.

"I'm just changing the rules again, that's all. The human mind is like a chess board, with moving pieces...and I can read your strategy in how your mind moves. You were going to hand me a worthless piece of paper, take the prize, and then have your men kill me, right?"

Krieger held the paper bearing his words and signature to the villain. "So clever, American. Here—take this as a gesture of goodwill on my part. I am a man of honor and I give you my word that your cousin will be returned to you—assuming he still lives. I hope he's hale and hearty but you have to know that I can't guarantee that. Unfortunately, I cannot allow you to leave this place without turning over the object."

The Puzzler glanced around at the other men in the room, all of whom were in the act of drawing their weapons. When the guns were all pointed in his direction, The Puzzler quickly calculated what options provided him with the best chance for survival...and came to the conclusion that he would most likely die if he resisted. Deciding that prolonging the game was not in his best interests, The Puzzler took the paper and slid it into a hidden pocket located at his right hip. When his hand re-emerged, it was clasped around a small object that Krieger couldn't see. "I guess I'll have to trust you, Captain. Here." He dropped the object into Krieger's palm, enjoying the look of shock on the Nazi's face.

It was a single bullet, forged of silver. "This...is this a joke?" the German stammered. "This is supposed to be a Ptolemaic tetradrachm. A coin!"

"It was a coin, my friend...it's just not one anymore." The Puzzler leaned forward and chuckled. "I found them in a vault hidden away in the attic of an Atlanta mansion—barely managed to get away before The Peregrine filled me full of lead[1]."

Krieger backhanded The Puzzler so hard that blood sprayed from the villain's mouth. "Talk sense!" he demanded.

The Puzzler spat on the floor and took a moment to probe the inside of his mouth with his tongue. A tooth was loose but hadn't been displaced. "The house was abandoned," he muttered. "But it had once belonged to a Frenchman that had moved to the South back in the

---

1 Max Davies, aka The Peregrine, is a masked vigilante that haunts the streets of Atlanta.

THIRTY PIECES OF SILVER

1890s before he died of a heart attack in 1907. The guy had ties to The Illuminati…I think that's where he got the coins. He had them melted down and turned into bullets—why, I have no idea. Maybe it was to hide them from the other members of The Illuminati—maybe he had one hell of a werewolf problem. All I know is those 30 pieces of silver were used to create twenty bullets." The Puzzler pointed at the bullet that Krieger still held. "Those things are *magic bullets*, Krieger. I know you thought they were powerful in their original form but I think that Frenchman made them even more potent by transforming them into these bullets. Now they're *weapons*."

Krieger sighed and looked down at the bullet. "Where are the rest?"

"Take that one back to your Fuehrer," The Puzzler replied, smiling and revealing a set of bloodstained teeth. "You'll get the other nineteen when I get my cousin."

CHAPTER II
MADNESS, IT SPAWNS FROM WITHIN!

LAZARUS GRAY FELT like his shoulders were about to rip from their sockets. He was dangling from the edge of a shattered window, some twenty stories above the hard streets of Sovereign. With a grunt, he tried to lift himself up, allowing his eyes to raise once more over the windowsill. His mismatched eyes—one a dull brown, the other a glittering emerald—immediately widened as he saw a frightening figure rushing towards him, brandishing a vase over their head. It was Veronica Beech, an alleged madam with her fingers in all sorts of perverse little crimes around the city.

Lazarus had been hired by a frightened couple named Lonnie and Darla Smith, whose teenage daughter had vanished into one of Beech's brothels. His investigation had led him to the madam's apartment at the Follies Hotel and when she'd gone off to dinner, he'd broken into her quarters in hopes of finding a clue to where the young Miss Smith might be…what he'd found in the spare bedroom would haunt him for many nights to come: Veronica was a murderer and she had the disgusting habit of saving the heads of her victims in brown paper bags under her bed. He'd found eight of them…and one of those heads had belonged to Lonnie and Darla's seventeen-year-old daughter.

Before he could alert the authorities, Beech had returned, having left behind her handbag. She had fought with the strength of a wild woman, knocking Lazarus back until he toppled right through the large bay window in her living room.

Lazarus grunted as Beech brought the vase crashing down upon his straining hands. The porcelain object shattered and so did one of Gray's knuckles, which bloomed with fresh pain.

"Die, you bastard!" Beech screamed, her face contorted by fury. That she was mad was beyond discussion—not only was it obvious through her actions but it was surely confirmed by the look in her eyes, which was one straight out of an Edgar Allan Poe story. This was the kind of woman that would be haunted at night by the still-beating heart of her victim or the tormented cries of a cat that she'd sealed up in the walls of her apartment.

The crazed killer began beating at Lazarus' hands with her fists, slamming them down like hammers again and again. Every time she made contact with his broken knuckle, Lazarus came close to losing his grip.

Knowing that his continued survival hinged on what happened next, Lazarus found purchase with his feet and then threw himself upward, using all the strength he had left to hurtle through the shattered window. His shoulder was slashed by a jagged piece of glass as he entered the apartment but this was forgotten a moment later as he slammed into Beech and knocked her over.

Gray pounced atop her, driving his knee into her midsection and knocking all the air from her lungs. He reached out with one hand and tangled his fingers in her hair. "Stop resisting," he told her, even though she was still fighting like a wildcat. He gave her scalp a yank and she stopped trying to pummel him with her fists. "Don't make me hurt you, Veronica. I don't want to do that..."

Beech seemed to calm down and Lazarus thought for a second that perhaps she would listen to reason—then he saw her outstretched right hand close around a piece of glass. Blood immediately began to flow as the makeshift weapon cut her palm but Lazarus was more concerned about what she intended to do with it. She slammed it into the meat of his upper leg and Lazarus was forced to respond in vicious fashion: he jerked her head forward and then drove it hard into the floor. He repeated the assault three more times until Beech's bloody hand fell away from the shard of glass and a glazed expression came into her eyes.

Lazarus clambered off of her, checking to make sure she was still breathing before he yanked the piece of glass out of his leg. Blood flowed easily down his pants' leg but Lazarus ignored it as he made his way to the building phone. He buzzed down to the apartment building's front desk, identifying himself and asking the clerk to call the authorities. When he was done, he set the receiver back on the cradle and turned back towards Beech. She still lay unmoving on the floor, a small pool of blood spreading in a semicircle from the back of her hair.

He sat down heavily on her couch, trying not to think too much about the uncomfortable conversation he would have with the Smiths later on. Being a father himself, he could only imagine the torment of losing a child.

The phone in the apartment suddenly began ringing and Lazarus thought about simply letting it go—but when it showed no signs of stopping, he rose and crossed back to the small table which supported it. "Hello?" he asked.

Static filled the line and Lazarus felt a prickle run down his spine. This was no call sent through by the operator…he had experienced enough of the supernatural to recognize it when he saw it. Or, in this case, heard it.

"Lazarus…" came the ghostly feminine response. Something about the voice sounded familiar but he couldn't quite place it…It reminded him of Miya's voice, with her slightly accented English. "I can't speak for long," she continued. "They're coming for you—they're going to try and break you."

"Who's coming? Who is this?" he demanded, knowing that he had no power to compel this person to answer either question.

The line suddenly cleared of all static, allowing Lazarus to hear the crystal-clear singing of a multitude of voices. It was beautiful, hauntingly so, and it took Lazarus a moment to recognize that the language being spoken wasn't English…it was a language that Lazarus had heard only once before. During his time with The Illuminati, Lazarus had gone by his birth name of Richard Winthrop. He had been unaware of the group's evil nature and had thrown himself into his work, delving into the mysteries of the world alongside his lover, Miya Shimada, and his mentor, Walther Lunt. The trio had traveled the globe seeking the truth behind many myths and legends—and on one occasion they had traveled to southeastern Turkey, where they had spent time with a group of Assyrians. These men and women had spoken Aramaic, the language that had once upon a time been the primary dialect of the Jews until Hebrew had supplanted it in the 7th century. Though he recognized the language, Lazarus wasn't fluent enough in it to immediately decipher the words that that were being sung—but the tone and style made him think of a choir. This was a religious song…

Static suddenly filled the line once more, followed by the click of someone severing the connection. He was staring at the phone in his hand when the door to the apartment flew open, allowing a small handful of police officers to stream into the room. They had made good time and Lazarus quickly made the decision that he wouldn't mention the strange phone call to them—it didn't seem related to Beech and her crimes. Besides, ever since Inspector Cord had died, Lazarus had played his cards closer to the vest than before.

Even as he was greeting the officers, Lazarus was mentally repeating the words from the song in his mind. As soon as he got back to headquarters, he would begin the laborious process of translating it… and then he would begin preparing for the arrival of whomever it was that was going to be coming to "break him."

LAZARUS GRAY'S HEADQUARTERS was located at one of the most famous addresses in Sovereign City—indeed, it was known by a large number of people all across the country. This was because the group that Lazarus belonged to was famous for helping those in need, no matter their race, political affiliation or ability to pay.

The headquarters of Assistance Unlimited was part of a city block that was entirely owned by Lazarus. What had once been an unassuming neighborhood had been transformed into the beating heart of Gray's law-abiding enterprise.

The centerpiece of his holdings was a three-story structure that had once been a hotel. Gray's associates used the first floor, while the second had been gutted and converted into one large room that was used for meetings, briefings, and research. The third floor was off-limits to everyone but Lazarus and his family, serving as their private residence. He lived there with his wife Kelly and their three-year-old son Ezekiel.

Facing the former hotel were several storefronts, all of which had closed down at the dawn of the Great Depression. They were now quite empty, though each was equipped with sensitive monitoring equipment that allowed Lazarus and his companions to keep track of every car or pedestrian that stepped foot onto Robeson Avenue.

Morgan Watts stood in the foyer, staring out of the glass doors that faced the street. As the oldest member of Assistance Unlimited, he often felt like he was a father-figure to some of his younger teammates. It was a role that he had reluctantly come to embrace. He'd given up hope of getting married, settling down and having a kid. The closest thing he'd ever have to a family all lived right here at 6196 Robeson Avenue.

And that was okay.

Always looking dapper in fine-tailored suits and a pencil-thin moustache, Morgan had long ago stopped giving off a "mafioso" impression. It had been hard to shake, given that he'd been a confidence man for the mob for nearly two decades before Lazarus had shown him a better path. Now he'd been on the better side of the law so long that few of his old compatriots were still in the criminal game. Most of them were either dead or in jail, many of them as a direct result of Assistance Unlimited's actions.

Morgan saw a familiar car drive by the front entrance of the building, swerving around the side to park in the underground garage. Lazarus was back—a little later than Morgan had anticipated. He absently reached for the pack of cigarettes he kept in his coat pocket...and then remembered that he'd stopped smoking several years back. Old habits die hard, he thought to himself.

"Morgan."

The blood in his veins seemed to cool, congealing to something hard and thick. That voice...it was impossible. It had come from behind him and it had sounded just like his older sister, Mary...she had died when she'd been fifteen years old, killed when a trolley car jumped the tracks and smashed into a crowd of people waiting to board it at the stop. Morgan had been just eight years old and he'd loved Mary so very, very much. At that point in his life he hadn't quite understood the way family worked and he'd fantasized about eventually marrying his sister and living happily ever after. She'd been his first crush.

"Morgan...please."

Slowly he turned, both excited and terrified by the prospect of seeing Mary again. He'd missed her for so very long, and yet...she was dead. He'd seen enough resurrections over the years—including Lazarus himself—to know that no one came back from the other side without paying a price.

There she stood, looking just like she had the day she'd died—pretty and thin, with just the right amount of curves to indicate that she'd blossom into a woman soon. Her dark hair hung around her shoulders, framing the milky white skin of her pretty face. Objectively he knew that her chin was a tad too sharp and her eyes just a little bit too far apart... but she was still beautiful to him. Her cream-colored dress stopped just above her knees and he could see the small scar on her left leg from where she'd fallen off her bicycle a couple of years before she died.

"Oh, my god," Morgan whispered. He was so engrossed in the sight of his sister that he didn't notice the ice forming on the windows behind him, or the way his breath now appeared in tiny clouds of fog. He shivered, thinking it was just from horror..."Mary? Is it really you?"

She took a step towards Morgan, reaching out with both hands. Her palms came to rest on his chest and he gasped—it felt like she'd plunged her hands into an icebox before placing them upon him. "Bad things are coming, Morgan. Terrible things."

"Are you...you're in heaven, aren't you?"

Mary smiled sadly. "It's not quite so easy to define. What comes after all this is...complicated. And simple. All at the same time!" Her smile faded as swiftly as it had arisen. "The gates of Hell are open. The pieces of silver are loose in the world. Beware Woland!"

"Woland? Who is—Mary!" Morgan cried out and reached for his

sister as she began to fade away, her body turning into a smoky silhouette before vanishing entirely. "Mary!" he repeated, turning in circles, in a vain hope that she might reappear.

She was gone and Morgan wondered if she had ever truly been there at all—or if he were simply going insane.

CHAPTER III
TEMPTATIONS

THE PUZZLER LEANED back in his chair, holding a cigar in his right hand. His ludicrous attire enhanced the strangeness of the situation—a masked super villain sitting in an expensively furnished penthouse, the soft strains of classical music playing from a nearby radio.

Seated across from him was a man who, despite the fact that he was dressed in a nondescript manner, was somehow even more unusual. Woland's appearance was described differently based on the observer— the clerk who signed him into the hotel last week would have said that Woland was short, with gold-plated teeth and a pronounced limp on his right foot. The Puzzler saw him as a man of enormous height with platinum crowns and a minor limp on the left foot. The prostitute that spent the previous night with him would have said he was absolutely normal in every fashion, save for a tendency to cruelty during lovemaking.

Woland wore a dark-colored suit with vest and jacket. A gold watch fob dangled out of one pocket but otherwise his entire ensemble was black-and-white in color. Woland held a glass of bourbon in his right hand and he raised it to his lips, taking a long sip before allowing the bottom of the glass to rest against his knee. "So how did the captain take the news of your bargain?"

"He didn't care for it—in fact, I think he wanted to put a bullet in my brain. I was able to convince him that if he wanted the rest of the silver, he had to play ball, though. He says he'll try and get my cousin."

"I have to confess," Woland said, swirling the alcohol in his glass.

"I'm surprised that you'd be so loyal to your family. It's admirable."

The Puzzler puffed on his cigar and gave a shrug of his shoulders. "When I was younger, I traveled back and forth between America and Europe. I always made time to see my cousin. We were close."

Woland smiled, knowing the full extent of The Puzzler's meaning. He knew many things that were unsaid by others—and in this case he was aware of The Puzzler's confused sexuality and the intense love affair he and his cousin had indulged in on so many occasions. Love was always a weakness, no matter what form it took. It made fools of all men. "The Nazis' love of bureaucracy means that they will be able to locate him easily enough. No matter how vile their atrocities, they keep meticulous records of all their actions."

"I hate the Krauts," The Puzzler muttered. "For every good one like my cousin, there are hundreds more that are good for nothing."

"Be careful, my friend…hating an entire group of people can lead to all sorts of problems later on. That's what's going on in Germany, after all—the Jews, the Marxists, everyone that doesn't fit in with the Nazi ideal. They're being segregated, abused, harassed…"

"Are you seriously comparing me to the Nazis?"

"Never! Simply giving you caution, that's all." Woland leaned back in his chair, watching as The Puzzler finished his cigar. He had found the man in a bar located near the Sovereign City Harbor. It was an establishment that catered to a certain type of clientele and Woland had found the villain in the arms of a swarthy Italian sailor…after suffering through The Puzzler's unnecessary explanation of how he had ended up there, Woland had informed the man that he had heard of his search for the Thirty Pieces of Silver. The Puzzler had immediately sobered up and offered to buy Woland a beer. Two hours later, The Puzzler was leaving Sovereign City on a plane headed to Atlanta, eager to retrieve the bullets from their attic home.

It said something that The Puzzler had not inquired more about why Woland was helping him. For someone who prided himself on being the smartest man in the room, he could be remarkably dumb sometimes.

The mysterious Woland was weaving a web, a tapestry, that would eventually include The Puzzler, the Nazi elite, Assistance Unlimited, and the forces of Heaven and Hell...

He smiled to himself as he drained the last of his bourbon. "What a wicked web we weave when first we practice to deceive," he murmured under his breath.

———∞∞∞———

THE VIENNA CENTRAL Cemetery had been opened on All Saint's Day in 1874 and from the moment the ground had been consecrated, it had been the center of controversy. The interdenominational nature of the cemetery had not been welcomed by all and fierce debates had broken out, led by the more conservative branches of the Catholic Church.

In the end, the cemetery had gone forward with a small Jewish section segregated from the rest of the graves and people were seemingly at peace.

But in the hearts of many, that debate still stirred and it had, in the mind of Alf Lindemann, taken on new importance as of late. He worked in the NSDAP Office of Racial Policy, or at least that was what it had been called since 1935. Alf had been there from the beginning—in 1933, it had been The Office for Enlightenment on Population Policy and Racial Welfare. Regardless of the name (and Alf tended to think the new one was a bit less unwieldy than the original), Dr. Walter Gross called the shots when it came to the Office's business. Their job was to organize and promote propaganda concerning the ethnic consciousness of the Aryan race. This was accomplished in many ways but Alf's primary focus was on the monthly magazine Neues Volk. It appeared on the surface to be a travel guide but sprinkled in amongst the vacation ideas were articles about eugenics and the ever-present "Jewish problem." Since the war had begun in earnest, it had produced such quality work as *Foreign workers are welcome but sexual relations with Germans prohibited."*

Other articles defended eugenic sterilization with photographs of mentally incapacitated children juxtaposed with those of healthy children. It also presented images of ideal Aryan families and ridiculed childless couples. After the inception of the Nuremberg Laws, it urged that Germans show no sympathy for Jews and presented articles to show Jewish life was still flourishing and the negative effect this was having on "proper" Germans.

Alf worked hard on those articles, though it turned his stomach to do so.

Alf Lindemann was a Jew himself—at least, one-quarter of him was, as defined by the Office's strict measures. And one-quarter Jew was enough to make him less than a true German.

Of course, no one in the Office knew about this—he had carefully doctored his own records and buried the truth about his grandmother's ancestry. Nevertheless, he knew the dichotomy that his life presented. By day, he was actively helping the Aryans around him depict his own people as being sub-human.

By night...Well, that was a different story.

Alf moved pensively through the grass, which was a bit long and unkempt. He wondered who was supposed to be maintaining it these days and why they had gotten so lax in their duties. Now was not the time to be shirking one's duties, after all. The Reich must be precise and productive in all things, as he himself had written in an article about Aryan work ethics.

Still, it barely mattered—winter was coming and when it did, the grass would die in the cold and bitter winds.

He finally stopped at a small family plot, consisting of two memorials surrounded by a low wrought-iron fence. His eyes moved over the larger: a wonderfully carved depiction of an angel, hands outstretched with eyes looking to the heavens. The name carved into the base of the statue read Magda Lindemann and the date indicated that she had died less than four years prior.

Alf held two flowers in his left hand and he bent low, placing them at the angel's feet. He cut a striking figure in his long black coat, buttoned over a dark suit and tie. He was only thirty-six years old but worry and stress had aged him, giving him the firm facial features of a man in his mid-forties. His hair was dark and thick, though his hairline had begun to recede slightly over the past few years. His body was hard and firm, like that of an athlete.

Magda had died at the hands of a Brownshirt, one that had drunkenly assaulted her on the streets of Berlin. Her last moments on Earth had been terrible ones, having witnessed her own baby being thrown to the ground, its skull shattered. The sexual and physical assault that had preceded her own death must have seemed like nothing compared to the horror of watching her child die.

Alf's gloved hands clenched into fists as his gaze moved on to the second monument, which bore the name Alfred Lindemann, Jr. Barely eight months old when he had died but he lived on in his father's memory. So full of life, with eyes that radiated an early intelligence. He could have accomplished great things.

Alf had been horribly broken by the deaths of his wife and son. For days after their funeral, he had been morose. The Brownshirt had escaped justice because of political connections but Alf wanted to see justice done...and if the authorities would fail him, his own body would not.

In his younger days, he had been a runner and a swimmer. He had kept himself fit, boxing on his days off. A strong body and a strong mind.

He had found out the man's name and address. After watching him for a time and learning his habits, he had waited for the killer to return home one evening and he had brutally beaten the man before slitting his throat. If the murder had occurred even a year earlier, there would have been a full investigation—but the so-called "Night of the Long Knives" had taken place only days later and the SA had been effectively dismantled and replaced by the SS.

Alf's fury had not dissipated after taking his revenge, however. Again and again, he had found himself wandering the streets at night, taking out his righteous fury against the very establishment that he served. He was a man of two lives: an Aryan writer and editor...and a

Jewish force of justice that the people in some areas had dubbed Nakam.

Taking his cue from the American vigilantes like The Peregrine and The Darkling, he had hidden his identity behind a white mask and a white suit. His actions were far less glamorous than his counterparts across the globe—in fact, many of the things he had done would have marked him as a killer and a criminal if he'd carried them out in places like Atlanta or Sovereign City, but here in Germany, he was the kind of hero his people needed.

He heard the crunch of boots nearby and he paused. Out of habit, he had surveyed much of the cemetery before coming to his family's graves. Without turning from his son's monument, he listened as the footsteps grew closer and then quieter, as if someone was taking pains not to be heard.

Tensing his muscles, Alf thought about the weapons hidden beneath his coat: brass knuckles, two knives, and a vial of poison. Of course, he was also capable of killing with his bare hands—and when it came to killing Nazis, there were definitely times when that was his preference.

The figure walking towards him caused him to relax and shift his expression from one of suspicion to forced gentility. Captain Albrecht Krieger was a frequent visitor to the Neues Volk offices—Krieger had been courting a young secretary that worked there and whenever he got the chance he dropped by in his full dress uniform, medals on prominent display. It was all rather ludicrous since Alf knew for a fact that the girl in question was a lesbian.

"Captain," Alf said, snapping a half-hearted Hitler salute in greeting. "What brings you to Vienna?"

"You do, Herr Lindemann."

"I'm afraid I don't understand…" Alf glanced about, expecting to see a squad of armed soldiers bursting from the shadows, ready to capture the fearsome Nakam.

"Your wife and son?" Krieger asked, gesturing with a gloved hand to the graves.

"Yes."

"A pity. My parents buried an older brother of mine. He died when he was thirteen and I was…seven, I think? My poor mother never recovered. My father stayed with her as long as possible but eventually he had to leave her. Thankfully he took me with him. She ended up in asylum—I would have hated to have seen her broken like that."

Alf shifted uneasily, uncertain what the proper response would be to a story like that. Eventually, he said, "I am sorry for your family's loss, Captain."

Krieger shrugged his shoulders. "Your kindness is noted, Herr Lindemann, but it is unnecessary. My mother was weak whereas you are strong. You miss your family and honor their memory but you have not allowed the loss to break you. Besides, it all worked out in the end. My father remarried and his second wife is far prettier than my mother."

"How…good…for him." Alf cleared his throat and pushed his hands deep into the pocket of his coat. "You came all the way here for me? May I ask why?"

"Yes. Are you familiar with a Jew by the name of Karl Harmatz?"

Alf blinked in surprise. "Uh…yes. I do—or did, rather. I knew him at university. Bright lad with a wicked sense of humor. It got him into trouble on numerous occasions."

"You were close with him?"

"I wouldn't say so, no. We knew each other and traveled in the same circles but I haven't kept in touch with him since we graduated. I didn't know he was a Jew," he added.

"I'm not surprised. Some of them can pass for a German pretty well—but if you spend enough time with them, you can usually tell." Krieger looked around as a small group of elderly men and women began moving through the gravestones, occasionally stopping to point and talk about people they remembered. "Harmatz was sent to a camp after he made several writings critical of the Fuehrer. For reasons that aren't important to you, I was told to retrieve him. Unfortunately, the camp's commander says that Harmatz escaped during a small uprising four months ago. I need to know where he might have gone, where he would be hiding out, who his associates might be."

Alf blinked in shock. "And you came to *me*? Surely there are people that know him better than I do! I don't even understand how you associated me with him in the first place."

Krieger tapped the side of his head and smiled proudly. "That is why I am a captain in the German military, my friend. I am clever. I saw in Harmatz's file that he attended the same university that I had overheard you talking about to Greta."

"And you came all the way here…just in the hopes that I might know him? There were many students there. I didn't know most of them."

"But you knew him, didn't you?" Krieger chuckled when Alf nodded. "I had a hunch that you would know him. He was a writer, a journalist…and so are you."

We're also both Jews, Alf thought to himself. "I'm not sure how I can help," he said. "I never knew him all that well…and it's been years."

Krieger put a hand on Alf's shoulder and gave it a squeeze. "Think about where you would go if you were in his shoes, mein Freund. If you were a Jewish journalist that was an enemy of the state…where would you go? You can't get out of the country without papers and you have no money with which to buy them. You are most likely in league with the Jewish underground or else you are living as a vagrant. Think like him—and help me!"

Alf paused, thinking that it wouldn't take much to imagine himself as a Jew hiding from the authorities… He wondered why Krieger would want Harmatz and he knew that if he could find him first, that would be best for everyone involved. "I'll do my best," he said, eliciting a smile from the German soldier.

"I have no doubt of that—and know this," Krieger removed his hand from Alf's shoulder and held up one finger. "If you do this job well, I can make sure that you get a promotion. How would you like to work on the Das Reich newspaper? You could work right alongside Herr Goebbels himself!"

Alf merely grinned—the idea of working alongside the Reich's propaganda minister was both disgusting and exciting. Disgusting because there were few in Germany more vile than Goebbels...but exciting because Nakam would dearly love to slide a knife through the man's throat.

CHAPTER IV
PROJECT: CICADA

MAJOR JOSHUA CARUSO was tall, with the sort of rangy build commonly found among polo players or swimmers. His hair was a reddish-blond and cut short, though a few strands of it fell over his forehead in a calculatingly haphazard fashion. He wore a blue suit, white shirt, and striped tie, all of which looked like they'd been custom-tailored to his specifications. There was an air of regal breeding about him but he was no soft scion of nobility—there was a hint of danger in his eyes and an obvious love of adventure.

As head of the United States' answer to the German Occult Forces Project, Caruso was frequently exposed to the bizarre: he had a team of psychics that worked for his agency; he had recently sat in on a séance to try and get military tactical support from no less than George Washington himself; and he had spent altogether too much time for his liking in the presence of Lazarus Gray and Assistance Unlimited. His was a peculiar career and one that had resulted in his own sister being terrorized by a killer known as Billhook... but despite all of this, he relished his work as the head of Project: Cicada.

Project: Cicada had reluctantly been signed into operation by no less than the President himself—because his Christian beliefs condemned much of the supernatural as being demonic in origin and he had no desire for the United States to go down that path. Caruso and others had pointed out the success that the Germans had found with the OFP, including the creation of multiple superhuman agents. The United States had plenty of superhumans—more than any other nation on Earth— but the vast majority of them operated without government oversight. Even the likes of The Fighting Yank occasionally made moves that rankled those in Washington… and attempts to create heroes that would "belong" to the U.S. government had mostly proven failures: either the experiments didn't succeed or those that were produced bolted from their controllers at some point, as The Black Terror had done[2].

Caruso pulled a cigarette case from his coat, retrieved a smoke from the case and lit it after tapping it against the table at which he sat. He had only taken a couple of inhalations before a feminine hand reached out and snatched the cigarette out of his hand.

Twisting slightly, he saw Samantha Grace looking at him with a frown on her pretty face. Slender, blonde, and graced with a peaches-and-cream complexion, Samantha was still a headturner, even after nearly a decade with Assistance Unlimited and the additional strain of motherhood. She wore a white dress now, cinched at the waist with a broad blue belt.

With a withering tone, she ground out the cigarette against the table and then tossed the butt into a nearby garbage can. "I'm pretty sure we've told you before—no smoking around here. Believe me, if Morgan can quit, you can, too."

Languidly rising from his chair, Caruso offered a smile and a slight bow. "My apologies. I smoke like a chimney so it's hard for me to remember when I'm around people that don't approve."

"That's probably the closest thing I'll get to an apology so…apology accepted." Samantha stepped around to the other side of the table and sat down. She waited until Caruso returned to his seat and then she brought her hands together atop the table and asked, "What brings you to Sovereign, Major?"

"No one else is joining us?" he asked.

Samantha pursed her lips and said, "Lazarus is being treated by Dr. Hancock in the medical section. Morgan took off to Tartarus to visit Abigail[3]. Eun is out on a job. Not sure where Bob is. Looks like you're stuck with me."

---

2 As depicted in Lazarus Gray Volume 3, "The Making of a Hero"
3 Tartarus is the name of the prison built by Lazarus to house those criminals whose abilities or intellect make it impossible for normal prisons to hold them. Abigail "Abby" Cross serves as the warden of the facility.

"I can think of far less pleasant hosts," Caruso said. He was looking at Samantha with those penetrating eyes of his and she got the feeling that he was used to most girls swooning under his gaze.

"Let's get to the point, shall we?" Samantha said. "Does Project: Cicada have a mission for us?"

"Our psychic division has been wracked with nosebleeds over some hoodoo that's going on in the netherworld. None of them can give me a solid lead on what's happening but they all agree it's potentially end-of-the-world stuff." Caruso withdrew his cigarette case, caught Samantha's narrowed eyes, and quickly put it away again. "Some of the most recurring visions have had to do with a sack of coins...a silver bullet... and the dead rising from their graves."

"Cryptic stuff," Samantha replied. "No clues about who or what might be behind these things?"

Caruso hesitated before answering. "A few of the psychics—not all of them—but three or four... they claim that they've seen images of Hitler, standing in front of a crucified Christ."

"That's...intense."

"If you think you feel that way, you should talk to the psychics that saw it."

Samantha leaned back and said, "That's not much to go on. I suppose we could keep an ear out for any chatter in the occult world but our best bet might be to have Abby try and do a reading of her own."

"That's kind of what I was hoping," Caruso admitted. "I do have one small lead, though...we put out word for anybody that was looking for silver bullets, the undead, anything that popped up in those visions. I got one guy that's part of The Puzzler's gang—he said that his boss took a job from the Nazis to round up some silver coins. Somehow the Puzzler got them to take a bullet instead."

Samantha let out a sigh, wondering how Bob was going to take the news. He and his young partner, Tim Roland, had fought The Puzzler about a half dozen times in the last few years—Bob always chafed when Tim claimed that the villain was their "arch-enemy" but Ronald

Harmatz was probably more deserving of that "honor" than anybody else that the Black Terror had fought.

Standing up, Samantha held out a hand to Caruso and said, "Thanks for the information. I'll let Lazarus decide our next course of action but I'd assume that Abby will be asked to use her abilities to find out more and Bob will spearhead a search for The Puzzler."

Caruso gripped her hand lightly and held on a trifle too long for Samantha's liking. "Why do you dislike me so much?"

"Besides the fact that you helped Billhook sell out all of our secrets? You humiliated my family...nearly ruined Eun's life...every one of us had something embarrassing smeared across the front page of the newspapers!"

Caruso flinched slightly before recovering. "That killer had my sister...I had no choice."

"I know—and that's the only reason I'm not punching you in your big, fat nose!"

<hr />

MORGAN IGNORED THE jeers of the prisoners as he moved through the halls of Tartarus. These men and women were some of the most dangerous individuals on earth and he took no small amount of pride in knowing that he'd helped put many of them in their current home. He tried to keep his eyes fixed straight ahead of him but he still caught glimpses of Doc Pemberley, El Demonio, and Alloy. The hatred that all of them felt for every member of Assistance Unlimited radiated from them, making Morgan's feet move all the faster. His well-shined shoes made click-clack sounds on the floor with every step.

He was relieved when he exited the main hallway and saw Abby's open office door up ahead. The facility's warden was a sight for sore eyes in more ways than one: the buxom brunette was absolutely gorgeous, with hair that fell in loose curls about her shoulders and a dangerous set of curves. She dressed to accentuate her assets, as well, with plunging necklines and form-fitting skirts—it made her look slightly less refined when standing side-by-side with Samantha but Morgan had never known any man to complain.

She was also a powerful mystic whose abilities had saved every member of Assistance Unlimited on more than one occasion. Her fiery romance with Jakob Sporrenberg—aka Eidolon—had nearly torn the team apart but when Eidolon had elected to leave Assistance Unlimited, the rest of the unit became tighter than ever.

Abby was seated behind a desk piled high with paperwork, a phone held to her ear. Morgan sat down when she gave him a smile and he realized that she was on the phone with Samantha—he could make out her musical tones through the receiver, though he couldn't understand exactly what Samantha was saying.

"I'll try and do a scrying in a little while," Abby said into the phone. "You were right about Morgan coming to see me—he just showed up. Maybe I'll try to convince him to help out. He can light the candles and then blow them back out," she laughed.

Morgan raised his eyebrows and waited patiently as Abby ended her call and hung up the phone. "What's going on?" he asked.

"Major Caruso stopped by and said his psychics are terrified about some new, hard-to-define threat. He thinks it might involve silver bullets, the risen dead, a sack of gold, and Jesus."

Morgan grunted. "If it involves Jesus, it's probably a sack of silver, not gold."

"What do you mean?"

"Judas was paid in thirty pieces of silver, remember? I don't remember anything about bullets in the bible but it's been a long time since Sunday school." Morgan took a deep breath, looking pensive. "Pieces of silver…"

"Interesting," Abby murmured. She grinned and leaned forward, giving Morgan an interesting view down the front of her dress. With her, he was never sure if she were so comfortable with herself that she didn't even think about such exposure or if she did it deliberately. "What's with the visit, Morgan? Need to interview one of my guests?"

"No, I'm actually here to see you." Morgan reached up and smoothed down his moustache. "I… saw something earlier today. My sister, Mary. She died a long time ago, when I was just a kid."

"I've never heard you mention her."

"It's not something I like to talk about. I loved her, Abby—and in all the years since she died, not once have I ever felt like she was watching me, or that her presence was with me, nothing like that."

"Where did this vision take place?"

"In the foyer of our home. She was right there, looking just like she did back when she died. She was scared…wanted to give me some sort of warning." Abby nodded for him to continue and Morgan knew he'd made the right decision in coming to see her—not only could Abby help determine if it was an actual supernatural event or if he were simply going crazy…but she was ready and willing to listen to his story without judging him for it. "She told me 'The gates of Hell are open. The pieces of silver are loose in the world. Beware Woland!'"

"You're sure that's what she said? Exactly?" Abby was rising as she spoke, her palms flat against the fronts of her thighs.

"Positive. I can see her in my head right now. You think it's related to what Caruso said, don't you? Thirty pieces of silver…that's what was in the bag. The dead rising…that's what Mary meant by the gates of Hell being open." Morgan sat forward. "But who's Woland?"

"That's what we need to find out," Abby said. "Right now."

———— ❦ ————

EUN JIWON DUCKED beneath the heavy fist that would have taken his head off if it had made contact. The Korean-American heard the shouts of the crowd—some encouraging him, others wishing him bodily harm—and the scent of the unwashed bodies nearly made him gag. Everywhere he looked he saw men waving dollars in the air, their faces twisted as they shouted at the top of their lungs. A few women were in the crowd, which pressed around Eun and his opponent in a circle, but they were all working girls and dressed as would have been expected.

Smoke filled the air and burned Eun's lungs. This fight club was an illegal affair, located at the harbor, and populated by the worst kinds of people. It wasn't the sort of place that a law-abiding man like Eun would normally be caught dead in but this was not his first trip here. Since his sexuality had been revealed by Billhook, he'd increasingly felt the need to prove his masculinity.

Eun drove a punch into his opponent's midsection, eliciting a grunt from the other man. Jim was much taller than the diminutive Eun, with a nose that had been broken multiple times and huge hands that looked like mallets. He was your typical bruiser and Eun made sure to use his speed to avoid the bigger man's blows.

Dancing back, Eun rocked forward, fists raised. Jim looked tired—and from the odor that wafted off of him, he was more than a little drunk.

"Come back here, ya Nancy Boy!" Jim bellowed, coming towards Eun with malice in his expression.

Eun felt stung by the homosexual slur and he responded viciously. He spun about and drove a kick into the side of Jim's head. As the big man stumbled, Eun followed up with a backhand to the man's chin and a final punch that once again shattered Jim's nose.

The big man swayed and then fell backwards, causing half the crowd to roar in approval and the other half to begin pelting Eun with verbal insults.

Eun ignored the pats on the back that he received as he pushed through the crowd, headed to the bar in the back. Willie, a bald-headed old man with liver spots on his scalp, grinned and slapped a glass of booze in front of him. "I knew ya would win, Eun. You're always linin' me pockets!"

"Thanks, Willie," Eun probed a tooth in the corner of his mouth. It had been loosened in a previous fight and he'd been afraid that one of Jim's glancing blows might have been its death knell…thankfully it was still hanging in there by its root. He tossed down the drink and grimaced

THIRTY PIECES OF SILVER

slightly—it was powerful.

"When are you going to be finished with all this?" a familiar voice asked from behind him. "Or are you going to keep getting into scrapes like this until one of these idiots finally kills you?"

Eun said nothing, not even when Eddie slid onto the stool next to him. Eddie had been his lover for several years and they were bound together not just by romance but by a deep understanding of one another.

Eddie looked unshaven and his eyes shone with worry. "When you weren't at home after my shift, I started asking around. Is this what you've been doing every night for the past few weeks? And to think I was worried you were running around on me."

"Keep your voice down," Eun said, glancing around the room. No one seemed to be paying them any mind and for that, he was glad. He didn't feel like defending his manhood at the moment...he was tired.

"Ashamed of me?"

Eun glared at his lover. "Stop it."

"Everybody knows you're a homosexual, Eun. That's why you're here, isn't it?" Eun started to stand but stopped when Eddie grabbed his arm. "I love you," Eddie said, lowering his voice to a whisper. "I'm worried about you."

Eun softened a bit, nodding. "I know. You don't need to be, though. This is just something that I feel like I have to do."

Eddie sighed. "Well...you either have to stop doing it or I'm leaving you."

"What?" Eun blinked in surprise and stammered, "You're not serious..."

"I am. It's one thing to risk your life with Assistance Unlimited. That has a point. It's helping people. This...this is just you trying to prove something to people whose opinion shouldn't matter anyway. Do you think any one of these guys that was patting your back feels any differently about queers than they did before? No, they don't!" Eddie leaned close and added, "If I'm going to stay up nights worrying about you, it's not going to be because you're out having barroom brawls. Understand?"

The two men stared into one another's eyes for a long moment and finally something inside Eun seemed to crumble apart…a wall of fear and self-loathing that he'd been slowly building up ever since Billhook's smear campaign had begun.

Eun finally let his shoulders slump and his hand came up to find Eddie's. He gave it a quick squeeze and said, "You win, Eddie."

"No," Eddie replied with a smile. "We both do."

CHAPTER V
KILL THIS LOVE

LAZARUS PULLED UP a chair, turning it around so that he sat it down backwards. He propped his arms on the back of the chair and watched as Morgan finished lighting the final candles. The flickering lights were arranged along the corners of a pentagram drawn on the floor in lipstick and the dim lighting cast strange shadows in the room.

Assistance Unlimited's leader had answered the summons from Abigail with great haste, knowing that she was not one to cry wolf when the circumstances didn't warrant. Samantha had come along, having filled him in on the way about Caruso's visit…as usual, it seemed that destiny was weaving a tapestry to force Lazarus down a certain path. The fact that Caruso's meeting with Samantha resulted in the realization that they needed Abby to perform a scrying—and that Morgan's vision coincided with the strange telephone call that he had received at Beech's apartment all pointed to something dangerous brewing on the fringes of reality.

Abby entered the room, wearing a gauzy white gown that emphasized her femininity. Though many people thought of Lazarus as an unemotional sort, he was most definitely a man—and he felt a quickening of his pulse as Abby passed by. The material was nearly transparent when she passed by the candles, rendering Abby virtually nude. The reaction from Morgan was more obvious, shown by a broad grin and a whispered "Oh, my…"

If Abby noticed the effect that she had on her male companions, she gave no indication. Instead she sat cross-legged in the center of the pentagram, raising her hands palms-upward in front of her. "Thanks for being here, guys—on the off-chance that something goes wrong, snuff out the candles, one-by-one. When the last one is out, I'll return to my body."

"Not that I'm complaining, but what's with the flimsy get-up?" Morgan asked. "I'm pretty sure I've seen you do this same ritual without putting on a nightgown."

"Given all the weirdness that you guys have prepared me for, I want to be comfortable…my appearance on the astral plane is whatever I make it but I don't want anything restricting my movement on this side of things. I could have gone completely nude but I decided to save my modesty."

Morgan glanced at Lazarus with the clear, unspoken question of, "*This* saves her modesty?"

Lazarus looked at Abby and asked, "What, exactly, are you going to try and do? Locate this Woland person? Try to draw upon whatever force warned Morgan and myself?"

"All of the above," Abby replied. "And then some…first thing I'll do is try to find any cracks in the framework of reality and look into those. If the dead are really going to rise from the grave, that means that there are some serious rifts between the realms of the living and of the dead. That should show up on the astral plane like a beacon."

"Be careful," Morgan said and immediately regretted it. Abigail knew more about this kind of thing than anyone else he knew—and she darned sure knew how to take care of herself.

Abby smiled, obviously not insulted by his concern at all. "Okay, gentlemen…silence, please." She leaned her head back and closed her eyes, intentionally slowing her breathing so that she could enter the state of consciousness that would allow her spirit to break free of its mortal shell. Though neither of the men could see it when it happened, she was successful and her soul lifted into the air, retreating into the formless void that existed between the world of man and the many arcane dimensions beyond.

ABBY FELT A chill run down her spine. She was standing in a misty landscape that was slowly taking form all around her. Her mystically-attuned senses had homed in on a rift and drawn her towards it…and now she saw before her, a jagged tear in the air, presenting her with a view to the world that lay beyond. She saw spirits, some lifelike in appearance and others more like something from a trashy pulp magazine, with rotting flesh and protruding bones. As she watched, these spirits approached the rift and crawled through it—immediately their forms turned to mist, fading from view. She knew what this meant: they were returning to the rotting shells that they had occupied in life… some of them would retain enough consciousness to almost seem normal, though their appearance would be horrific. Most, though, would be driven insane by either their time in the afterlife or the insanity of being restored to a decomposing body.

The images swirled and Abby found herself no longer standing in front of the open portal…she was confused since she had not willed the change. Spinning about, she noticed that her appearance was also a surprise: she wore what looked like a nun's habit, stained with blood. A heavy weight around her waist caused her to look down to see that a small bundle was tied to her belt. Uncinching it, she reached into the pouch and felt several familiar items—drawing them forth, she stared at a handful of silver bullets.

"Thirty pieces of silver, that's all it took—for a man to betray the son of God."

Abby looked up to see that once again her surroundings had been altered. She was still dressed in the bloody habit but now she stood at the foot of a hill, at the top of which stood three large wooden crosses, each with a body hanging limply from them. Standing at her side was a nondescript little man wearing an odd-fitting suit and holding a cigar. His face was nearly hidden beneath a bristly white beard. "Are you trying to tell me that these bullets…were forged from the coins given to Judas?"

"I'm not trying to tell you anything, Miss Cross." The old man looked at her and she saw a smile appear beneath his whiskers. "Just like I'm not trying to tell you that you're looking at Jesus up there and that this is

Golgotha, which in Aramaic means 'place of the skull.' Christians often give it another name of course—"

"Calvary," Abby said and the old man nodded in approval.

"Good girl!" he beamed. "And do you know who I am…?" Before Abby could answer, he added, "Let's just say that I was right here when Jesus had his moment of doubt and pain. I even whispered in Pilate's ear to make sure that the deed was done just right. 'Wash your hands of the whole thing,' I told him. He actually thought he could."

Abby shook her head. "You're not the devil."

"How do you know?"

"Because I've faced demons and sorcerers alike that have claimed to be Lucifer himself…and in the end, Assistance Unlimited has trumped them all." Abby dropped the silver bullets back into the sack at her waist and asked, "So what's your game, Woland?"

"Ah, you know one of my many names." Woland tossed aside his cigar and pointed up at the dying form of Jesus. "For God so loved the world that he gave his one and only Son, that whoever believes in him shall not perish but have eternal life. Bullshit."

"You're avoiding my question."

Woland looked at Abby and his enigmatic smile reappeared. "The temptation must be so great for you…constantly skirting along the edges of true power, always drawing back right before you cross over into black magic."

Abby slashed her hand through the air, sending a wave of ectoplasmic force into Woland. The little man was sent flying, landing in a heap at the foot of Christ's cross. He stirred slowly and for a moment Abby thought he was groaning in pain—but then she realized that it was hoarse laughter emanating from him.

She moved closer to him, summoning another burst of eldritch energy but paused when Woland stood up, brushing off bits of ectoplasm from the front of his suit. He was completely unharmed by her attack, which should have affected him not only on the astral plane but in the "real" world, as well.

"I've flayed people for doing less than that, my pretty," Woland warned. He began speaking, his voice growing more and more strident with every word until eventually spittle flew from his open mouth and his eyes took on a red, maddened glare. "You want to know what game I'm playing? I'm doing nothing less than turning the world of men into a suburb of Hell! Those bullets are potent things, charged with the greatest of sins…and I'm going to make sure that they end up in the hands of mankind's most dangerous fool! I've torn down the walls between the living and the dead so that everyone can learn the awful truth: God is no longer watching over you. He gave up and moved on to other things long ago. There's nothing left for you but to kill one another; to rape, to steal, to rut in the dirt like the filthy mongrels you are!"

Abby shook her head and her look of confidence returned, which seemed to incense Woland. "You're definitely not the devil—you're trying too hard." She spun about and began to walk back down the hill. Over her shoulder she said, "I'll tell Lazarus that we've got another power-mad despot to take down and his name is Woland. Same story as always."

Woland suddenly appeared in front of her, blocking her path. "Don't taunt me, little witch! I'm only telling you these things because I fully expect Lazarus Gray to try and stop me—and I want him to know that much of this is his fault. It was he that fought his way out of the afterlife and it was he that traveled back and forth to Dread Carcosa[4]! As much as anyone, it was he that weakened the barriers between the living and the dead! All of his past sins are now coming home to roost! I want you to tell him this!"

Abby drew back a fist that was flaming with magical fire—she drove it right into Woland's face, letting it burn through astral flesh and bone. Her hand came out the other side of his head before she yanked her arm back, allowing the mutilated form of her enemy to topple over. As Woland fell, their surroundings shifted once more and Abby found herself standing in the middle of a burning synagogue. A masked figure in white was standing nearby, a knife in his hand—Abby recognized him as Nakam, the German freedom fighter. Nakam was shouting

---

4 These dramatic events took place in volumes 6 and 7, respectively.

something but she couldn't make out his words...a second later his body was wracked as bullets tore through him, spilling crimson all over his white suit.

Abby didn't need to be told what kind of bullets were ripping her friend apart.

They were silver.

—⚬⚬⚬—

ALF MOVED THROUGH the streets of Berlin, a dryness in his mouth. The city had changed so much in such a short amount of time...the early days of what eventually became the war were heady times for most Germans. The victories in the Sudetenland had practically been bloodless affairs and it had lulled many citizens into thinking that the Fuehrer could do no wrong. He was going to take back all the honor and prestige that the Treaty of Versailles had stolen from Germany.

Now, though, the entire world was at war and the notion of an easy path to Nazi domination was no sure thing. Many Germans had grown accustomed to the idea of an alliance with Fascist Italy, but the Japanese? There were many that had been happy that Hitler had declared war on the United States in the aftermath of the Japanese attack on Pearl Harbor.

All of this, of course, was from the perspective of the "pure" German. Those poor souls that were political dissidents, communists, homosexuals, mentally deficient or, worst of all, Jewish had known for quite some time that not all was well in the Fatherland.

Cinching his coat tighter around himself, Alf ducked down an alley, ignoring the stares he received from several thin men huddled together. What their business was he didn't know nor did he care. He sensed their suspicion of him and knew that whatever they were up to, it was something that the authorities would have frowned over.

Carry on, mein Freunds, he thought to himself as he hurried past. He stopped outside a door hidden in the side of a brick building. A sign overhead directed visitors to the front entrance but Alf ignored it, rapping on the door and casting another glance at the men at the other end of the alley. They had returned to their private discussion and had, if anything, moved even closer to one another. Alf was certain that they were trading some sort of verboten goods with one another.

The door opened a crack and Alf saw a woman's face appear. She had dark hair, prominent cheekbones and an ashen complexion. A large mole above the left corner of her mouth caught his eye. In a hoarse voice she asked, "Yes?"

Rather than answering verbally, Alf reached into his coat and retrieved a piece of paper. He held it up for her to look at and then quickly returned it to his pocket. It was a Hebrew symbol that meant God and the woman stared at him for a moment more before opening the door and ushering him inside. The interior of the place was filthy— dirt lined every surface and there was an unpleasant odor in the air that reminded Alf of spoiled cabbage.

"What is your name?" the woman demanded.

"You are Helga?"

"Yes. And you?"

Alf noticed for the first time that one of the woman's hands was kept partially out of sight and he realized that she was holding some sort of weapon. With no hesitation, he gave her a fake name, one that he used from time to time when he didn't want his real identity to be compromised.

She blinked without recognition, as he had known she would. She'd ask around about him later and receive information that said he was a Jew in hiding, just like her. There were a lucky few in the major cities that had been able to bribe the right officials or forge the correct documents to hide their Jewish ancestry. These papers would not hold up to deep inspection but if they avoided any acts of suspicion, these Jews hoped to hold out for the end of the Nazi regime, assuming that ever came.

Unfortunately for these poor souls in hiding, many of them found themselves unable to turn a blind eye to their brothers and sisters in need. As such, many of them engaged in activities that, if discovered, would mean their incarceration or death. This woman—Helga Klum—

was supposed to be the owner of a small delicatessen. That was true enough—but what kept her busiest was the flophouse she ran in her attic, allowing Jews to crash there for a few days before they vanished deeper into the Berlin underworld.

"You need a place to stay," she said. It wasn't a question. "If you have money, that is best. If you don't, I will allow you to sleep here in exchange for cleaning around the restaurant."

Alf allowed his glance to drift over the filth. Evidently she was rather lax in enforcing *"payment."* "Actually, Fräu Klum, I am here seeking information. A friend of mine recently escaped from a prison camp and I believe he's here in Berlin. I was hoping you could help me find him."

New suspicion bloomed in Helga's eyes and she took a step away from Alf. "If you were really friends, I'm sure he'll get in touch with you. One of my rules is that I never betray the confidences of those that stay in my home."

"I don't mean him any harm," Alf replied. "In fact, I want to help him. Powerful people are after him and I don't know why…I want to find him before they do and make sure that he's safe."

"You want Karl Harmatz, don't you?"

Alf blinked in surprise. "How did you—? Have there been people here already? Looking for him?"

"No. If the authorities had found us here, I'd be locked up in a camp just like he was." Helga wrapped her arms about herself and continued, "Before he left, he told me that someone would come looking for him. He said that his location was just another puzzle to be solved and that he knew someone that was very good at those. Does this make sense to you?"

"No," Alf replied in all honesty. "I don't think he was referring to me." Alf reached for her, gently touching her arm. "I'm a Jew," he said, unconsciously lowering his voice, as if the Gestapo were lurking in the very next room. "Every day and every night, I live in constant fear of being found out. I will do nothing—*nothing*—to risk your work here or Karl's life."

Helga stared into his eyes and for a moment he thought that she was peering into his soul, seeing all of his secrets. He wanted to look away but he was afraid that she would think he was a liar if he did. Finally, the old woman gave a curt nod and pulled her arm out of Alf's grasp. "He was given papers and told to visit Hoffman's Butcher Shop. Herr Hoffman rents rooms above his shop and Harmatz was going to take one."

"I know that shop—I sometimes buy from him." Alf blinked in surprise and asked, "Is he a Jew, as well?"

Helga straightened, as if something in his question was insulting to her. "No…and neither am I. Not all Germans share the Fuehrer's madness."

Alf felt a rare smile touch his lips and an absurd urge to hug this filthy old woman nearly overwhelmed him. "Thank you, Fräu Klum, for reminding me of that fact. It's so easy to fall into the trap of thinking that everyone is falling in line with the government's decrees but there are many like us—keeping to the shadows to preserve our survival but doing all that we can to resist."

"I am no hero," Helga said shortly. "I simply cannot stand aside and allow others to be persecuted for nonsense like the myth of the Jewish threat."

Giving a bow of thanks, Alf left the establishment. He was eager to find Karl and he knew that Hoffman's would be closing soon. If he arrived too late and the butcher refused him entry, it might be up to Nakam to pay an unannounced visit to the apartments upstairs.

CHAPTER VI
PUZZLEMENT

BOB BENTON TOOK several deep, calming breaths. He was a gentle man by nature but as soon as he put on the leather attire of The Black Terror, he had a tendency to let loose with his violent inner urges…in the past, this had brought him perilously close to murder. Thankfully, he had learned to temper his anger with meditative techniques taught to him by both Lazarus and Abigail.

He stood at the foot of a flight of stairs, leading up to an apartment being rented by The Puzzler. With him were two of closest friends: Lazarus Gray and Samantha Grace.

Lazarus was wearing a white shirt with the sleeves rolled up, a vest, khaki pants and an over-the-shoulder holster. The holster was empty at present as Lazarus held his favored pistol—a .357 Smith & Wesson Magnum—in his right hand.

Samantha's outfit mirrored Gray's in many ways—a white shirt (though hers was short-sleeved), khaki jodhpurs and black leather riding boots that stopped just shy of her knees. She held a weapon of her own in her hands—a hardened rubber truncheon. There were many times that she went into combat unarmed, knowing that her excellent judo skills would serve her better than any gun. In this case, however, she opted to wield a policeman's-style club

Lazarus glanced over at The Black Terror and gave a nod, indicating that Bob could lead the way whenever he was ready. The hard-hitting hero began ascending the stairs, overly conscious of every creak that resulted. Though he wasn't truly human—he was the product of a government experiment to "create" their own heroes—Bob felt a surge of adrenaline much like what he suspected his companions were feeling.

The Puzzler was a frequent sparring partner of his and both the villain and Bob's young partner, Tim, considered The Puzzler his archenemy. Bob thought the very notion to be absurd...and more than a little bit troubling. If he did his job right, and the justice system did its part, he shouldn't face any foe enough times to warrant a feud.

They passed a concerned man on the stairs. The man wore a heavy coat since rain was in the forecast, and held a suitcase against his chest as he allowed the members of Assistance Unlimited to squeeze past. The poor fellow's eyes fixed on Samantha's truncheon and Lazarus Gray's pistol and they heard his hurried footsteps as he rushed away from whatever violence was about to ensue.

As they reached The Puzzler's apartment, Samantha crept forward and put her ear to the door. It was generally agreed upon that she had the best hearing of the bunch and it was only a few seconds before she nodded and stepped back.

"He's in there," she whispered.

The Black Terror raised a booted foot, feeling the scabbard he wore on his hip shift. Despite the fact that his fists could punch through steel, he carried a cutlass with him at all times—sometimes there was really nothing better than stabbing something.

Or some*one*.

The Terror's kick splintered the door into a dozen shards and elicited a high-pitched scream from inside the apartment. Samantha and Lazarus rushed in, each taking a different side of the door, weapons at the ready. The Black Terror came straight in through the middle, knowing that his toughened flesh would be adequate protection against most small-arms fire.

What they saw brought all three to a halt. The Puzzler was there, all right, but he was hardly in a position for combat. He was kneeling on the floor, dressed only in a domino-style mask and an altogether too-short robe. With him on the floor, also mostly undressed, was a young woman with a bobbed hairstyle and far too much makeup. Only a quick glance at what the woman was quickly trying to cover up between her legs gave the understanding that this was not a woman at all but a pretty man in drag.

The Puzzler let out a roar of indignation and, while the heroes were still gaping in surprise, seized hold of a wine glass off the floor. He smashed its rim against the floor, leaving a jagged rim. Seizing his companion by the shoulder, he yanked the transvestite against him, pushing the glass hard against the man's throat. Blood bubbled against the pressure and The Puzzler grinned. "Lower your weapons or the bitch gets a new smile!"

⎯⎯⎯ ∞∞∞ ⎯⎯⎯

TO SAY THAT Bob was somewhat "square" was to put it mildly. The jazz musicians that had originated the slang term used it to describe people that were a bit out of touch with modern music and culture. Bob had only just gotten used to Eun's homosexuality—seeing a man in women's makeup was enough to boggle his mind.

He could see that The Puzzler's mind was working, calculating the odds. The man was known to most as being adept at leaving behind complex clues but that was a terrible understatement when it came to his abilities—he saw the world as a series of puzzles to be solved and he was able to break things down to their components to best assess them. Bob had only been able to defeat him because he was, by nature, a very straight-ahead fighter. The Puzzler would set up a brilliant series of diversions, all of which The Black Terror would ignore in favor of simply busting through every phase of the man's scheme and ultimately punching him in the face.

In this case, such direct action might end up in The Puzzler's hostage being killed so Bob held up and allowed Lazarus to step forward, raising both hands upward. He slowly holstered his gun and said, "There's no need to hurt him. We just want to ask you some questions, that's all."

"Questions? About what?"

"A man named Woland…and thirty pieces of silver."

The Puzzler's eyes widened briefly and then quickly narrowed. What he did next was so shocking that both Bob and Samantha were completely gobsmacked. He slit the young man's throat, sending an arterial spray of blood into the air and then, even as he tossed the body towards the feet of Lazarus Gray he drew back his arm and hurled the murder weapon at a mirror located just over Samantha's shoulder. She instinctively ducked out of the way but the broken drinking glass shattered upon impact. Shards went flying in all directions—and The Puzzler had correctly calculated each one. Samantha cried out as she felt a large piece catch the back of her head, sending warm blood down the back of her neck…and The Black Terror grimaced as a small bit of shrapnel caught him in the eye, one of the few places where his dense flesh provided no additional protection. Bob's hand flew up to his injured eye and he began carefully trying to remove the shard without causing further harm to himself.

Lazarus reacted with lightning-quick speed, however—somehow, it seemed that he had predicted the villain's maneuver, as unlikely as that seemed to Bob. Even before the drinking glass shattered against the mirror, Lazarus was in motion, throwing himself over the falling corpse and tackling The Puzzler. Where Lazarus had been standing, a large enough piece of glass to have proven fatal crashed to the floor.

The Puzzler let out a grunt of surprise when Lazarus sent him toppling backwards. He hadn't anticipated this and that both distressed and amused him—people were normally so predictable.

Lazarus wrapped a hand about the villain's throat and said, "Give up or I promise you that you'll regret it."

"Oh, I think you're wrong about one thing," The Puzzler gasped out. "You're the one who's going to regret touching me." The villain twisted about, proving himself to be quite limber—he threw his legs up, his ankles wrapping about Gray's head and pulling backward. Lazarus was so surprised by the action that he lost his grip on the Puzzler's throat.

The villain rolled out from beneath the hero, scrambling back to his feet. His robe had fallen open, revealing a pair of satin underpants that was the only bit of clothing protecting The Puzzler's modesty.

Springing forward, The Puzzler swung a roundhouse punch towards

Lazarus' face but the hero blocked the attack and answered with a quick blow to the villain's midsection. As The Puzzler gasped for breath, The Black Terror—blood still oozing from his wounded eye—grabbed him by the left arm. The leather-clad vigilante yanked The Puzzler's arm upwards and The Puzzler cried out in pain.

Lazarus glanced over at Samantha, who was kneeling next to the transvestite. She had rolled the man over on his back and was checking for a pulse, more concerned with helping him than tending to her own bleeding scalp. "How is he?" Lazarus asked.

Samantha looked up with disgust in her eyes. "He's dead. Poor kid couldn't be more than seventeen or eighteen."

"You've been just a burglar up to this point but now you're a murderer, Ronald," The Black Terror hissed into his enemy's ear. "Even though the Sovereign legal system has an open door policy, I think I might be able to convince Lazarus to toss your sorry ass into Tartarus!"

The Puzzler ceased his struggles and Lazarus could see genuine fear in the man's eyes. Apparently stories of Tartarus had spread throughout the underworld. "How about I answer your questions in return for going easy on me?" The Puzzler asked, willing to deal now that he saw no easy escape from the scene.

"That sounds like a plan," Lazarus said, his face betraying no indication of his inner thoughts. "First, though—we need to know about this young man you just killed. He has family, I'm sure."

"He's a runaway. I picked him up at Father Clive's. It's a bar on the east side that caters to…a certain clientele."

"Do you know his real name?"

"He told me to call him Marla. Trying to track down his family probably wouldn't be a good idea," The Puzzler couldn't help but grin. "From what little he did tell me, his homelife wasn't very good."

The Black Terror gave the villain's arm another twist. "You're a sick one, Ronald. I had no idea you were into little boys. And in dresses…!"

Samantha stood up, having closed "Marla's" eyes. "I'll make a mental note to check in on this Father Clive place," she said to Lazarus.

Nodding, Lazarus gestured for The Black Terror to release the villain. Reluctantly, Bob did so but he remained close enough to grab his enemy again if need be.

"Ronald Harmatz," Lazarus said, putting emphasis on the man's real name. He knew that The Puzzler hated it when people refused to use his pseudonym. "I want to know how you first met Woland and what his ultimate plan is…and I want to know anything and everything you can tell us about the silver bullets."

The Puzzler winced as he rolled his shoulder, trying to get the kinks out after The Black Terror's manhandling. "Can I at least put on some clothes? Standing here in my shorts is a little distracting."

"You can manage, I'm sure. Start talking."

The Puzzler took a deep breath before moving towards the couch. He sat down and crossed his legs, making a show of cinching his robe in the front. "The first thing you should know is that you don't want to mess with Woland. He's an old man with a lot of secrets and a lot of power. Second, it's not just me and him you have to worry about anyway. The Nazis are involved." The Puzzler smiled at The Black Terror. "Hitler himself is at my beck and call these days, BT."

"Does he like little boys in makeup, too?" Bob retorted.

Ignoring the jibe, The Puzzler paused a moment before launching into his tale. "It all began with my cousin…"

———◦◦◦———

THE PUZZLER'S STORY was one that made Bob a trifle uncomfortable. Though the villain left many details unstated, it was clear that during his teens he had traveled overseas many times and that his relationship with his cousin went beyond mere familial friendship. They had lost touch with one another after the rise of the Nazi party and the growing tensions for Jews within the Reich. When The Puzzler had learned that his cousin had been taken to one of the

Nazi camps, he had considered trying to return to Germany to break him out but not even his keen intellect saw a way for that to turn out successfully.

Months passed before The Puzzler was approached by a German officer named Krieger that had heard of his unusual skill in solving problems. The German explained that the Reich was interested in accumulating objects of a religious or mystical significance and that they were having difficulty locating nothing less than the 30 pieces of silver paid to Judas to betray Christ. At first the Puzzler had scoffed at the very notion—working for Nazis was bad enough but surely this was nothing but a wild goose chase...but the promised money was enough to make him reconsider.

Even with his amazing skills, The Puzzler hit a series of dead ends in his pursuit of the coins. It was only after he'd given up all hope and decided to drown his sorrows in booze and illicit sex that he'd met Woland. The old man, whose appearance seemed to vary depending on who was doing the looking, had interrupted The Puzzler's lovemaking (just as Lazarus had done, the villain had pointed out—"This is becoming a terrible habit," he droned). Woland had offered to buy his drinks for the evening and claimed that he knew of The Puzzler's recent fruitless searches...searches that he could point in the right direction.

Pointed in the direction of an old plantation house in Atlanta, Georgia, The Puzzler had finally located the thirty pieces of silver...only to find that they were in a different form than he'd expected. Melted down and transformed into bullets, the pieces of silver were now a potent weapon—even though he lacked any mystical ability of his own, The Puzzler could feel the energy pulsing from these things. Holding more than one in his palm at once gave him a weird thrill that traveled up and down his spine.

Upon returning to Sovereign City, The Puzzler went to see Woland to thank him for the tip...and he discovered that the old man was full of wonderful ideas. One of his suggestions was to use the silver bullets as leverage to free Ronald's cousin from the prison camp where he was held. After calculating the odds, The Puzzler had moved forward with this plan and he was now waiting to give the rest of the silver to Krieger upon the arrival of his cousin in America.

When he was done with his story, Samantha looked at Lazarus before asking The Puzzler, "And what is Woland getting out of all this?"

"What do you mean?" the masked man asked, looking annoyed—and Samantha got the sudden impression that he had never before considered this seemingly obvious question.

Samantha gave a shrug and said, "Some stranger shows up out of nowhere and he gives you the location of the silver...and then he encourages you to use it as a bargaining chip with the Nazis. If he knew where the silver was, why didn't he get it himself? How did he know about your cousin? Why is he getting involved in all this at all?"

The Black Terror openly scoffed, saying, "What kind of moron are you to not ask these questions yourself?"

Lazarus held up a hand, quickly adding, "It may not be his fault. Woland sounds like a potent magician—it's conceivable that he cast some sort of glamour on Ronald and that's why these things didn't occur to him."

The Puzzler pursed his lips, turning his mind over all that was being said. When he spoke again, he declared, "It must have been some sort of spell, like you said. That only begs the question again, though: *why*? He hasn't asked for anything from me and I can't fathom how he'd benefit from me getting my cousin back...or from the Nazis getting the silver."

Lazarus pulled up a chair and sat down. "Abigail—another member of our team—has met Woland. He gave her a story about being the literal devil and wanting to completely tear down the wall between the living and the dead...to create literal hell on earth. I think he was using you as a conduit for some reason. He wants Hitler to get these bullets but is either unwilling or unable to complete the transaction himself. He needed you to do it—as for the angle with your cousin, I think it's nothing more than an attempt to delay the transaction. He wants Hitler to have the silver but *not yet*. So he's having you draw it out."

"Clever," the villain replied. He looked at Lazarus and asked, "I suppose you want to know where to find him?"

"Yes. I assume you've been to his home?"

"More than once." The Puzzler stood up. "May I come along?"

"Don't do it," The Black Terror murmured, glancing at Lazarus. "We can't trust him. Let's just throw him in Tartarus and be done with him."

Lazarus stared at The Puzzler for a moment, locking eyes with the other man. He saw the villain wilt under his gaze but the man refused to look away. "No…I see where you're coming from, Terror, and I respect that you're much more familiar with him than I am but I'm curious why Woland chose to approach him of all people. I think his desire to uncover the answers himself will keep him loyal to us—to a point. Beyond that, I trust that you'd be willing to hit him really hard if you needed to?"

The Black Terror grunted. "Without hesitation."

Nodding, Lazarus stood and said, "Ronald, get dressed…and then let's go pay Mr. Woland a visit."

CHAPTER VII
THE CRIMSON LADIES

BRUNO HOFFMAN GROUND out his cigarette beneath his boot. It was awful with very little tobacco flavor…already things were growing scarce because of the war and he could not afford the sort of cigarettes that he had once enjoyed. Sighing, he removed his bloody apron and tossed it into the open door behind him before pulling the door shut and locking it. He glanced up at the curtained windows above his shop—a few lights were on up there and he shook his head. He'd warned them all about keeping the candles and lamps turned down… the last thing anyone needed was attention from the authorities, after all.

Bruno was pushing fifty and growing heavier by the day—but the weight on his shoulders felt much greater than the bulk he carried in his midsection. He was not a Jew but he had known many and had even seriously considered marrying a Jewish girl when he was younger and slimmer. He would have stayed out of all this, however, if he hadn't personally witnessed an old Jewish man beaten to death outside the butcher shop by a couple of Gestapo officers just over two summers ago. Bruno had reacted instinctively when the attack began, stepping outside and demanding to know what was going on—the old man had been one of his steady customers, after all, frequently coming in to buy beef and lamb on a regular basis. One of the Gestapo had angrily whirled on him and asked if he truly wanted to get involved…and to Bruno's everlasting shame, he had shaken his head and returned to his store. He had stood there behind the counter as the man was murdered right there in the street.

Not long after, Bruno had heard rumors of a clandestine network designed to help hide Jews and, despite the tremendous risk to his own life, he'd tracked down some of the people involved and offered the rooms located above his shop. It had done a little to help with the guilt he still felt but he knew it would take the rest of his life to truly absolve his soul, if it would even then.

He set off down the road, unaware that his movements were being observed from the shadows. Thankfully, it was not an agent of the Gestapo that was observing him—it was a figure dressed all in white, from his jacket to his slacks to his tie. Even the mask he wore to obscure his face was as silvery as the moon itself.

Nakam, the living embodiment of revenge, was once more stalking the night. He crept from the darkness, his eyes flicking left and right to ensure that no one was observing him as he headed towards the butcher's shop. On the right side was a fire escape and he reached up to grip hold of the bottom. It squeaked a bit as he pulled it down to the ground but he was taking the stairs so quickly, two at a time, that no one above had time to react, even if they had heard the noise.

Nakam paused at the first window he came to—the shades were drawn tight and he had to crouch and remain still for a moment to make out the silhouettes within. The form he saw was decidedly feminine and he moved on, despite a momentary urge to remain…the shape was quite enticingly built.

The second window was easier to spy into, for its owner had neglected to pull the curtains all the way closed. Nakam saw a lean male figure sitting in a worn wooden chair, reading by candlelight. Despite the gauntness of the body and the effects of aging, Alf was certain that this was the same Karl Harmatz that he had known years before.

Alf rapped on the window with gloved knuckles and had to stifle a grin at the way Karl jumped. He felt bad for thinking it funny—Karl was probably in fear for his life, after all. Still, there was something comical about the way the other man scrambled to his feet so fast that his chair toppled over and crashed to the floor.

Karl stared at the masked man looking in his window for a long moment before setting aside his book and cautiously approaching. He unlatched the window and pulled it up, asking, "You're him, aren't you? Nakam?"

Crawling in through the window, Alf nodded and said, "I'm surprised you've heard of me."

"Are you joking? Everyone in the community knows of you—the specter that strikes back for Jews everywhere! Some people say you're a ghost or an agent of God or even a myth." Karl grinned, showing several missing teeth, and Alf inwardly flinched. Karl had once possessed a beautiful smile that had been capable of stealing young girls' hearts. "I confess that I thought you were just a story fashioned to give us hope. Did you really kill seven Gestapo in Coburg?"

"It was eight—but who was counting?" Nakam looked at the disheveled living quarters and once again felt badly for his fellow Jews. Karl was living in an area barely large enough for an adult, with rat droppings on the floor and a chamberpot that was filled to near overflowing. Food sent up from the shop below consisted of strips of meat too fatty to sell—some of it lay near the discarded book, covered in flies.

"Why are you here?" Karl asked, his voice dropping. "Do the Nazis know about this place...?"

"No," Nakam said. His voice was distorted by the mask he wore, giving it a slightly inhuman aspect. He usually enjoyed the effect it had on others because he rarely interacted with anyone other than an enemy—but he regretted the way that Karl reacted every time he spoke. "The Germans are very much interested in you, Karl, and not just because you managed to escape from the camp. They're going to your old associates, people you haven't met in years...and offering them rewards for information leading to your capture. They don't normally go to this much trouble to recapture a single Jew. Any idea why they think you're so valuable?"

"I've always thought I was the most important person around but I'm surprised that they'd agree," Karl replied, displaying the same wry humor that Alf remembered from University. He picked up his fallen chair and set it upright, offering it to Nakam. When the masked vigilante shook his head, Karl sat down and exhaled. "There's only one thing that I can possibly think of that might explain it but even that's a stretch."

"Tell me."

"I have a cousin...an American. His name is Ronald. We were very close when we were younger. The last time I talked to him, he told me that he'd embarked on an...unusual...career." When Nakam said nothing, Karl pushed on, revealing, "He's a costumed criminal. Calls himself The Puzzler. From what I understand, he's fought The Black Terror more than once."

Nakam turned over those facts in his mind. He couldn't see why an American criminal would be of importance to Krieger but that had to be it—nothing else in Karl's background seemed to fit. "We need to get you out of here," he said. "I can cover for you, cover your tracks, but the best thing is to get you out of the country. Your mention of The Black Terror gives me an idea of where we can hide you, assuming we can get you to the United States. I've worked with Assistance Unlimited before."

Excitement swelled in Karl's eyes but it was quickly dampened when the sounds of gruff voices below, followed by the shattering of a door, reached his ears. "Oh, no," he whispered. "You must have been followed...!"

Nakam moved to the window and looked out—a military vehicle was parked outside and he could see several soldiers staking out positions on the perimeter of the property. Booted feet were now headed up the stairs leading from the shop to the apartments. "They must be here for someone else, not you. I'm certain I didn't lead anyone here."

The apartment next door suddenly exploded in a cacophony of sound—the scream of a young woman, no doubt the one that Nakam had briefly spied upon. Male voices shouted for the woman to surrender but within seconds this was followed by gunfire.

"Leni," Karl gasped. "She made propaganda flyers and put them around the city."

"They'll come to the rest of the apartments next," Nakam warned, grabbing Karl by the elbow and leading him to the window.

"We can't go out there," Karl hissed, seeing the armed men below. "We'll be killed!"

Nakam's grip on Karl's elbow tightened. "Look to the left," he hissed.

Karl did as he was told, turning his attention to one of the soldiers waiting outside—the man was suddenly enveloped by a flapping red cloak and the flash of light catching on a silvery blade made him jump. The soldier went down, just as similar attacks took out his comrades. Within seconds, these hardened agents of the Reich had all been killed—by faceless, hooded figures in scarlet.

"Are they...with you?" Karl asked hopefully.

Nakam's silence was all the answer Karl needed. The faceless vigilante moved away from Karl, crossing quickly over to the door. There was silence next door...in fact, the entire building was now as quiet as a tomb. The hooded figures were like nothing Nakam had ever seen before—the speed with which they moved...! And the cloaks were so all-encompassing that the gender and ethnicities of the killers were obscured.

Kneeling in front of the door, Alf saw a shadow pass under the door—and a brief, tantalizing flash of crimson cloth.

"They're here," Nakam whispered. "The men in red."

"What are we going to do?" Karl asked.

Nakam's hand vanished into his white jacket and when it came back into view he wore what looked like spiked knuckles. A quick depression of his thumb against the side of the device caused a thin blade to jet forth from the back. Now he was ready for mayhem. "We fight," he told his old University friend.

THE DOOR TO Karl's quarters swung inward, revealing four crimson-robed figures. The cloth covered them from head to foot, leaving only kohl-darkened eyes visible. Scarlet gloves held curved short-swords and the wielders moved with absolute silence, their robes not even rustling as they entered the room.

The room was completely swathed in darkness and the four intruders paused, looking about in the gloom. They were obviously expecting to find an emaciated, terrified Jew—and not a spectral figure dressed in white and wielding a deadly weapon. When Nakam sprang from the shadows, his blade singing a silent song of devastation, all four of his enemies jerked back in surprise.

The closest figure would never make another move as a living being. Nakam's knife embedded itself in their throat and when the masked man yanked it free, a spray of red spattered to the floor, just narrowly missing his shoes. One of the things that fed the stories that Nakam was not a living man but rather a ghost or a spirit of vengeance were the tales that his white suit was never marred by even a single drop of blood.

Even as their companion fell twitching to the dirty floor, the other three figures in crimson recovered and were eagerly meeting this unexpected threat. They fought well as a trio, boxing him in and striking in concert so that he was unable to fend off all their attacks. The one directly in front of him stabbed with their blade towards his face and he blocked the blow with his own knife, but the two on either side of him struck hard—one caught him just under his ribs, the other in his shoulder. Neither drew blood, however, as they uncovered one of his many secrets: Alf was not nearly as well-built as his suited body would imply. He had a swimmer's body underneath it all but when attired as Nakam, he appeared to be a boxer or low-level weightlifter. The truth lay in the fact that beneath his clothing he wore padding—it restricted his movement somewhat, though he had trained with it for so long that he felt naked when fighting without it. This padding provided protection from small arms fire and bladed weaponry.

Nakam drove an elbow into the nose of the attacker to his left, ducked low and swiped with his blade towards the midsection of the one in front. He was pleased to see red of a different sort drip to the floor as a result. The enemy to his left tried to bring their blade down atop his head but they missed as he rolled towards them, knocking their legs out from under them and sending them toppling down into their ally's blood.

It was at this point that Alf realized that all of his opponents were women. Karl, despite being told to stay out of the way, had moved forward and yanked away the hood hiding the face of the dead intruder, revealing a youthful female face dotted with freckles and reddish hair. Upon seeing this, Nakam noticed that the one whose robes had been slashed by his blade had staggered back in an attempt to gauge the severity of their wound—and he caught the distinctive sight of the underside of a female breast on display as they yanked up their robes and felt for the hole left by Nakam's blade.

Alf had little regard for men that assaulted women but he was no fool, either. These opponents of his were hardly dainty little flowers—they were obviously trained fighters who intended to kill him. Thus, he spared them no mercy when he sprang back into the thick of the battle.

The one he had previously wounded looked up just in time to see death come crashing down upon her as Nakam's blade was stabbed right into her heart. He yanked it free just as one of the others leaped onto his back, wrapping strong legs about his midsection and raising her knife high in the air. Before she could bring it down, Nakam took several steps backward and drove her hard into the plaster wall. She grunted and Nakam quickly spun her about as her remaining companion rushed forward. Nakam heard the woman on his back cry out as her ally accidentally stabbed her in the back, a blow intended for Nakam.

He turned again as he felt the one that had been clutching on to him drop to the ground. She was bleeding badly from the wound given her by her supposed friend. Nakam squared up, ready to face the fourth and final member of their group.

To his surprise, however, he saw her eyes go wide as a wooden chair came crashing down upon the back of her skull. She staggered under the unexpected assault and Nakam finished her off with a stab to the throat—which left him staring with appreciation at Karl, who held the shattered remnants of his chair in his hands.

"You don't listen very well, do you?" Nakam asked.

"You're welcome," Karl replied with a grin. He gestured towards the one surviving crimson-garbed woman, the one that had received a knife-wound to her back from her own partner. "Are you going to finish her off?"

"Not without questioning her first." Moving back over to the window,

Nakam looked out and saw no sign of movement below. Could it be that these four were the only ones remaining? Had their allies outside left to avoid possible detection, confident that their friends could finish off whatever mission they were here for? "Have you ever seen people like this before?" he asked, looking at Karl.

"What? No! Of course not!"

"It can't be coincidence that both me and them come to this location at the same time…but I don't think they're working for the Nazi that's leading the pursuit of you, either. So that means you're important to multiple people, Karl."

"Maybe they're friends of my cousin?"

"Possibly." Nakam gestured towards the window. "Keep watch. Let me know if you see any more of them down there." Kneeling beside the last of the women, Nakam jerked her hood off and seized her by her hair, pulling her to a kneeling position with his knife pressed against her throat. This one was in his mid-thirties, he guessed, with severe features and shoulder-length brown hair. Her eyes were cold—she was a killer by nature. "Name?" he demanded.

"I gave up my own name years ago," came the reply. A small spray of blood came forth as she coughed. "I'm one of the Crimson Ladies— that's all you need to know and all I'll tell you."

Nakam resisted the urge to sigh. He had met a few people in his time that were genuinely able to back up words like that…but most men and women had a limit to what they were able to endure. It was nothing more than big talk because when it when to came torture, nearly everyone had a breaking point. The real question was how far Alf was willing to go—he had certainly done foul things to people that deserved that and worse but he didn't know the full backstory of this "Crimson Lady" and he wasn't sure exactly what kind of punishment she required.

"All right, Miss Crimson Lady…what's the name of the person in charge of your little club?"

The woman cast her eyes towards Nakam and her chin tilted upward a bit as she proudly declared, "I serve at the request of no less than the

Lady Lilith herself, she who was formed of clay at the same time as her husband Adam. Unlike the weak-willed Eve, who was created to be subservient, Lilith refused to bow down before her husband. She walked out of Eden and became the mistress of carnality, the empress of night, and the mother of monsters."

"I see movement," Karl said.

Nakam nodded. "How many?"

"Three. They just stepped from the darkness—they're looking up at the windows but I don't know if they can see me. I'm sure they're wondering what's taking the others so long."

Nakam pressed the blade harder against the woman's throat, drawing blood. "If you want to live, answer me this: why are you here? Why is Karl so important to you?"

"I'll tell you because nothing you can do will matter in the end— we are an unstoppable army led by a powerful woman." The woman grinned as she spoke, revealing blood-tinged gums and teeth. "Lilith saw in a vision that this Jew was a crucial piece of some dark plan...she saw one of the dark lords of Hell, a sodomite in garish clothing, a man with one green eye and one brown, and she saw a faceless man all in shadowy circles around him. We were told to capture him and bring him before Lilith so she might learn more about him."

Nakam grunted—so their presence here merely meant that they wanted the same information that he did: why was Karl so essential to so many people? He didn't know anything about the dark lord of Hell that she'd mentioned but he was obviously the faceless man...the sodomite in garish clothing was Karl's cousin, The Puzzler...and the man with the mismatched eyes was Lazarus Gray. He suspected that he was not going to get anything else useful from this nameless woman so he terminated the discussion by slicing her throat open from ear to ear.

As she fell over, twitching, Nakam turned back to a gaping Karl and asked, "There's an attic, isn't there?"

Nodding slowly, Karl answered, "Yes. It's full of things for the shop below."

"There's a window?"

"Yes...but no way off the roof," Karl stammered.

"Let me handle that." Moving towards the door, Nakam motioned for Karl to follow but the man seemed strangely hesitant. "What's wrong?"

"You murdered her."

"I didn't see you having any concerns about her friends that I killed."

"They were fighting you! She was...she was helpless."

"She was a murderer, Karl...if we'd left her alive, she would have told her companions about us. The less they know, the better. Now— are you going to stay behind and take your chances with the Crimson Ladies or are you coming with me?"

Visibly taking a deep breath, Karl followed after his faceless savior.

KARL HAD FULLY expected to find himself witness to more bloodshed but Nakam surprised him by successfully leading them both to safety. The attic was full of boxes and smelled of mildew but the window opened easily enough, providing the two men with access to the roof.

While Karl stood nearby, shifting his weight from foot to foot in a sure sign of anxiety, Nakam pulled out a small length of rope from the inside of his white jacket. He tied one end of it around the chimney stack and the other around his waist. He then rappelled down the back of the building, looking just as smooth as Luis Trenker in *The Holy Mountain*. Once at the bottom, Nakam gestured for Karl to pull the rope back up and do the same. He did, though his heart was hammering so badly that his hands shook and he nearly wet himself before his feet touched solid ground.

Nakam quickly untied Karl and said, "The Crimson Ladies entered the building while you were coming down. We can make our escape now."

"You really think you can get me to the United States?" Karl asked, allowing himself to be led by the elbow into the darkening gloom.

"Yes…but don't fool yourself into thinking the danger is over once we're there. I have a feeling that these Crimson Ladies—not to mention Captain Krieger—don't give up easy."

CHAPTER VIII
DUEL WITH THE DEVIL

THE FERGUSON HOTEL had been erected in 1937 and quickly gained a reputation for being the ritziest joint in Sovereign City. The lounge regularly featured jazz musicians like Fletcher Henderson, Cab Calloway, and Benny Goodman, and the rooms were furnished in a sort of over-the-top opulence that appealed to guests hungry to put the so-called Great Depression in the rearview mirror. Not even the growing clouds of War in Europe and the Orient had put a damper on the hotel's growing buzz…and Pearl Harbor hadn't caused the hotel's owners to worry even a trifle.

Far more concerning to Derrick and Patricia Cabbagestalk, the wealthy couple that had sunk their life's savings into The Ferguson and been rewarded many times over, was the phone call they'd received earlier tonight from no less a personage than Lazarus Gray himself. The leader of Assistance Unlimited had informed him that a very dangerous individual was currently renting the penthouse suite of The Ferguson and that Gray and his compatriots intended to question this gentleman— and he felt it wise to alert Mr. Cabbagestalk to the potential for violence. At Gray's advice, the hotel had evacuated the two floors beneath the penthouse—it was difficult to do such a thing without attracting undue attention but Cabbagestalk was appeased somewhat when Gray offered to pay the displaced patrons' tab in the lounge for the duration of their time out of their rooms.

Derrick was with those guests right now, watching as they drank his booze and listened to the band. He was a big man, tall and broad-shouldered, but he'd quivered in his boots when The Black Terror had passed him in the foyer. Lazarus Gray was the only member of

Assistance Unlimited to take notice of Derrick, though, as he'd passed, he'd stared right at the hotel owner and nodded, as if he knew exactly who he was looking at.

Most people didn't even know who Derrick really was—he and Patricia were both Negroes, having come by their fortune by hard work and a little bit of good luck. Derrick did most of his business dealings by phone and Patricia said that his ability to "talk white" had been instrumental in their success as hotel owners. If the wealthy men and women that stayed at the Ferguson had any idea that they were staying at a "Negro hotel," things would have gone south in a hurry.

He hoped to hell that his hotel wasn't about to be turned into some kind of warzone...if it was, he was sure that Gray would give him money for it but this place was more than just a business to him—it had become home. Hell, he and Patricia lived on the fourth floor in a private suite!

His wife seemed to sense his thoughts. She reached over and put her hand over his, giving it a squeeze. "They got this, honey," she whispered, leaning in to give him a quick kiss on the cheek. "Lazarus Gray is a *hero*. He called ahead and had us get all these people to safety, didn't he?"

"Yeah, which is worrisome," Derrick replied gruffly. "He knows there's gonna be shooting or something. Maybe even a good old explosion or two."

"Relax, honey."

"I'll relax when they've come back downstairs with Mr. Woland in tow. Until then, I'm gonna keep right on drinking."

———⚬⚬⚬———

THE ELEVATOR OPERATOR quickly pulled the gate closed behind the exiting members of Assistance Unlimited. The poor man had been nervous the whole way from the ground floor up to the penthouse, keeping his eyes cast downward. The proximity of these notable figures sometimes made people act differently than they normally would—some gushed out praises and asked for autographs, but many reacted as this fellow did: Lazarus Gray and his companions were a magnet for danger and wherever they went, violence was sure to follow.

The team fell into position without Lazarus saying a word. They all knew their roles and functioned well together. The Black Terror and Lazarus would be the first ones into the apartment—Lazarus held his pistol, the Terror brandished his cutlass. Following them on the right would be Eun and Abigail—Abby had already prepared several spells that she thought would prove useful. On the left would come Morgan and Samantha, both armed with handguns loaded with silver-tipped bullets that had been soaked in holy water. These six men and women knew they were about to confront a man that claimed to be no less than Satan himself but not a one of them felt the slightest twinge of fear: they had fought the likes of Jack-in-Irons, Satan's Circus, and Murder Unlimited. Along the way they had conquered death itself and always risen to fight another day.

On this particular day, however, they were joined by another—The Puzzler stood behind them all, eager to confront the man that had used him as a patsy in some obscure scheme. He was unarmed and had been told to stay out of the combat—which suited him just fine. He was a thinker, not a fighter, after all.

Lazarus gave a subtle nod to Bob and received a cool grin in return. The Black Terror drew back his free hand, balled it into a fist and slammed it hard against the penthouse door. The stout wood splintered immediately, the shards flying into the apartment and loudly announcing the arrival of Assistance Unlimited.

Hurrying inside, the members on the sides dropped to shooting stances, ready to fire. Lazarus and The Black Terror strode into the center of the room, where Woland sat calmly beside a radio. The man appeared to Lazarus like a heavyset fellow in his late sixties, with a bushy white beard and large eyebrows. He wore wire-rimmed spectacles and a white suit with vest and tie. The Black Terror saw someone quite different—he viewed Woland as a remarkably fit fellow in his early forties, dressed in a tattered safari-style shirt that revealed his bronzed chest and well-muscled arms. To Bob, this was no old man but a male of intense physicality, ready to trade blows with any and all.

"Well, well, well," Woland said, setting aside the drink he had been holding. He reached over and turned off the radio before turning to face the intruders. "To what do I owe the pleasure of your company, Mr. Gray?"

"Don't act surprised to see us," Lazarus replied. He moved closer to Woland, pointing the barrel of his gun directly at the man. "Your little talk with Abby was virtually an open invitation."

Woland grunted in reply, a smile appearing beneath the bristly white whiskers that Lazarus saw on the man's face. "It was just as much of a warning, actually. You've been a very bad boy, Lazarus…you like to think that you've made a lot of amends for your past with the Illuminati but the truth is that you've continued making a mess of things, only now you do it under the cloak of goodness."

"I want you to tell us the full truth about what's going on. Why do the Nazis want the coins? Why did you use The Puzzler instead of going after them yourselves? What's the point of tipping us off to you? And why did Morgan and myself receive those visitations?"

"Well, you certainly are asking for a lot, aren't you?" Woland gestured to the couch and chairs arranged around the room. "I should think you would want to sit down…this might take a while."

"Stand down, everyone," Lazarus said and his teammates reluctantly did as he asked. He had seen this man's type before—he was dangerous, yes, but not until he had his moment in the sun and could reveal his "genius" to all. Woland wanted to talk…and Lazarus would let him.

For now.

⁂

"**B**EFORE WE CAN deal with the pieces of silver, we must go back to the beginning…the very beginning. I trust you are familiar with the story as laid out in the Book of Genesis?" Woland poured himself another drink, offering the bottle to others when he was done.

All turned him down but Morgan persisted by adding, "Are you seriously going back to the dawn of creation with this story?"

"In order to fully appreciate what comes later, you must understand what led to it," Woland replied. "The bible that most people know is not the full story—it has been revised, it has been edited, there are things that have been left out...the Catholic Church, in particular, has censored many apocryphal texts. What I am about to tell you includes many details from those forbidden books."

"Before Eve, there was Lilith—Adam's first wife. She was his equal in all ways and refused to submit to his dominion so she was cast out of Eden, her name scrubbed from the bible because she went against the tradition of the church in that women must obey a man and women were in a lower position than men. The original text from the King James Bible of Genesis 1:27 says "And God created man in his own image, in the image of God he created him; male and female he created them." This clearly shows that God created both man and woman at the same time. Lilith had been created equal to Adam. While she would have had different organs inside—the reproductive organs—in general terms they both had the same strength and character. When it came to sexual relations, she did not wish to simply lay beneath him—she also wanted to lie atop him. Adam refused this, thinking it placed them on equal footing. The apocryphal book of Genesis states "Why should I lie beneath you?" He asked. Lilith replied, "I was also made with dust, and therefore I am your equal..." As Adam tried to force her to obey, Lilith, angry, pronounced the name of God, and left."

Samantha cleared her throat and asked, "I thought woman was formed from one of Adam's ribs?"

"That was Eve," Woland answered. "She was not created of the same stuff as Adam...or Lilith. She was merely a piece of Adam given life. From the beginning, Eve was secondary to her husband, something that Lilith never was."

"Okay, so Lilith didn't know her place, so to speak," Morgan said. He held up a hand when both Samantha and Abby shot him disapproving looks. "I'm speaking from Adam's point of view, not my own, ladies. So she heads out on her own...where does she go? There were only two people in the whole world at the time, right"

"Two humans, yes," Woland replied. "There were other creatures, however—one being the demon Samael. She took up with him and bore him children, monstrous things that were wicked and cruel, ugly in form and spirit. God looked upon Lilith and grew angry—he cursed her and all her offspring. The apocrypha states, 'She liked the man's reproductive liquid very much, and she always walks to the point of seeing where she has fallen. All the liquid of man that does not end in the matrix of the wife is hers: all the seminal liquid that man finds wasted throughout his life, whether by adultery, by vice, or in sleep.'"

"Bullshit," Abby hissed. Eun, standing near her, blinked in surprise at the anger in her voice. "It's just the church trying to condemn women for having the same sexual appetites as men. Lilith enjoyed sex so she's a demon. Eve was a 'good' girl that liked it missionary position and that's who women are supposed to aspire to."

Woland chuckled. "There are many that would agree with you, Miss Cross. Lilith has been portrayed as an evil figure by many within the church, assuming you can find any that would admit to her existence at all. Much of it is indeed as you say, men have often coveted the sexually permissive woman but are quick to condemn her."

"They all want the virgin slut," Abby continued. When she saw the confusion on Samantha's face, she explained what she meant and she saw Samantha begin to nod as she did so. "Men want the girl they can take home to mother…the good cook and the faithful wife…but in the bedroom they want her to suddenly turn into a harlot, ready to drop to her knees and do whatever they want. Worse yet, if she's not capable of being both virginal and promiscuous, they go looking for what they're not getting elsewhere and then blame their partner for not being all things to them."

"I feel like we're getting off-topic here," Morgan murmured.

Woland shook his head. "I think your witch is on to something, Mr. Watts. Many women felt the same…and a group of them began to worship her. Lilith does not age, you see—she is just as lovely today as she was at the dawn of humanity. Her cult still exists even today… and it was her cult, the Crimson Ladies, that dug up the thirty pieces of silver after Judas buried them, just prior to his suicide. They were in possession of the coins for quite some time before deciding that the evil that had come to taint them was too great and too powerful—Lilith's followers tried to destroy them but found that this was not possible. When melted, they would inevitably reform, when thrown into the ocean, they would wash back onto the shore. Eventually they decided to scatter them around the globe—and for centuries they were never completely brought together. Their power was still used for many ne'er-do-wells but the full threat was seemingly dispelled...until The Illuminati began slowly accumulating them, grabbing one here and another there. It took them nearly two hundred years but eventually The Illuminati was successful. When the last of the thirty pieces was finally brought back to its siblings, it fell to a man named Eobard Grace[5] to prevent them from being used to plunge the world into a new Dark Ages. In 1893, he wrested them away from The Illuminati and gave them over to a friend that fled with them to the Southeastern United States. Before they hid them away, Grace and his friend melted the coins down and used the silver to make bullets. Since they were not destroyed but merely transformed, this has not been reversed in the years since. It hindered attempts by mystics and psychics to find them, however..."

"Until you told me where to find them," The Puzzler pointed out.

"You make Lilith sound like a hero here," Morgan said.

Woland glanced at The Puzzler but spoke to Morgan. He asked, "How so?"

"You talk about how evil these coins are and how dangerous they are...and then you talk about Lilith trying to destroy them and hide them so nobody can use them. I thought she was just as bad? Why didn't she try to use them to take over the world or something?"

Lazarus answered before Woland could. "Woland didn't say she was evil—he said that she'd been *portrayed* as evil by the church."

"Exactly!" Woland said with an approving nod. "She is not perfect by any means—she is as flawed as anyone else—but she is not the monster that the church would like you to think of her as." He stared

---

5 This is an untold adventure of the hero depicted in The Family Grace: An Extraordinary History

off into space, looking as if he were remembering things long past. "I suspect that she might be either friend or foe to you, depending on the situation."

"I think we understand the background well enough now," Lazarus continued. "The pieces of silver were cursed by Judas' actions, Lilith's followers got them after his suicide, they scattered them, the Illuminati put them back together, and then Eobard Grace stole them, melted them down into bullets and left them with a friend in Atlanta. Now: why did you lure The Puzzler into this and how do the Germans play into it all?"

"The Germans' role in this should be obvious," Woland answered. "You are very familiar with the Geheimnisvolles Kraft-Projekt, also dubbed The Occult Forces Project, or OFP. They are obsessed with locating objects of mystical importance for use by the Reich. There are many within the military that despise the OFP and want to court Hitler's favor on their own. Captain Albrecht Krieger learned that the OFP was on the hunt for the cursed coins and he undertook it on behalf of the military to find them first. I keep a close eye on things that relate to the damning of human souls and the coins have that effect on people…so when I discovered what he was up to, I made sure to steer him towards The Puzzler, whom I had identified as a useful patsy."

"Why? Why me…?" The Puzzler demanded. "I don't appreciate anyone playing me for a fool…or tampering with my mind!" He angrily tapped the side of his skull with two fingers. "This is my greatest tool! Do you understand that? If I can't trust my own brain, I have nothing!"

Woland actually looked a bit apologetic as he explained, "I was unfamiliar with you until I began closely studying Lazarus Gray… through him I was led to examine the rest of Assistance Unlimited. It was because of The Black Terror that I discovered you. I have a knack for seeing the weaknesses of others and when I discovered that you had a Jewish cousin of a certain sexual persuasion, and that he was being held by the Nazis, it all fell into place." Woland rose from his chair, limping slightly as he moved around his seat, facing his guests.

"The warnings sent to Lazarus and me," Morgan asked, "Those came from you?"

"No… Those came from the spirits that were leaking through from the other side," Woland replied. Seeing the expression on Morgan's face, he added, "Yes, you spoke to your sister's spirit."

Samantha reached out and lightly touched Morgan's arm but he was staring at the floor, moved by the revelation.

"Go on," Eun urged, eager to see how all this was finally spun together.

Woland continued speaking, obviously relishing the moment—he was in command now and his audience was nothing if not rapt. "If the coins are used to commit another atrocity against an innocent, a wave of supernatural energy will wash across the planes of existence. The fragile wall between the realm of the living and the dead will be shattered and humanity will be plunged into a veritable Hell on earth. I couldn't touch the coins myself...the nature of the curse upon them says that only mortal men and women may use them for evil. I needed a proxy—and since my goal was to get at Lazarus Gray, I had no real desire for the Nazis to ever possess them. The Puzzler's demands for them to release his cousin is just a red herring, something to distract them...and to help lure Assistance Unlimited right here, right now."

The Puzzler frowned, even as Assistance Unlimited tensed for an ambush. "You don't have all thirty coins, though—you said they need to be together. I gave one to Krieger."

"No, you gave *a* coin to Krieger...but not one of the thirty. I swapped it out before you handed it over to him. I knew that neither you nor he would be able to tell the difference between an actual piece of the original thirty or one that I had cursed myself."

"So hand them over now," Lazarus said, his mouth a thin line.

"I'm afraid I can't do that," Woland purred. "You see, I've already given them to someone else...and they're going to use them to commit a terrible, terrible crime. In fact, they're probably doing it right now. And then...then Sovereign City will become a literal hellhole. The dead will rise and then spread across the globe." Woland began to laugh, an unholy sound that chilled the blood of even the hardened heroes of Assistance Unlimited.

CHAPTER IX
AN UNSPEAKABLE SIN

KELLY EMERSON GRAY was a stunningly beautiful woman. Standing nearly six feet tall and possessed of flowing red hair, she looked like a modern Amazon. Her curves were enough to unsettle even the most experienced of playboys but her glittering green eyes contained a sensitivity that made people feel that they could trust her. Giving birth to her son three years before had given her body a slightly softer appearance than normal for awhile, but she was now back to the flat tummy and athletic muscle tone that she'd carried for most of her life.

It wasn't just her physical attributes that made her desirable, however. A graduate of Sovereign City University, she held doctorates in both archeology and anthropology. Despite the fact that she was a woman in a male-dominated field, she was regarded as one of the leading minds in archeology and had been the obvious choice to succeed her father as curator of The Sovereign City Museum of Natural History when he'd finally retired after a lifetime of service.

As spouse to Lazarus, she'd seen her fair share of weirdness and as a result she was often quite paranoid, anticipating threats around every corner. Thus, it was nice to occasionally have days like today, when she could relax and just simply enjoy her job.

Today the museum was playing host to several church youth groups—the facility was alive with the sounds of laughter and the squeals of children. Most of the kids were between the ages of eight and fourteen, with a smattering older or younger than that. Kelly stood outside her office door, watching them as the groups milled about on the first floor with their chaperones.

"They're great, aren't they?"

Kelly glanced to her left to see Dorothy Davis, one of the museum's secretaries, standing nearby. Dorothy was an attractive woman of mixed race—she could, and often did, pass for white. She was intelligent and hardworking—and had become Kelly's best friend at the museum. "They really are," Kelly said. "Won't be too many years before Zeke will be out there with them."

"Oh, please! Your little boy is only three! Don't rush him—you'll miss these years when he's feeling himself as a teenager." Dorothy held a cup of coffee and she took a sip before saying, "Don't want to alarm you but I told Henry to check out a few guys that came in the front door a few minutes ago. They looked like they were up to something."

Kelly kept her face neutral but she could feel her blood begin to race. Henry was the museum's security guard—a little on the beefy side, he had retired from the police force and was a popular figure in town. He knew his business but Kelly was enough of an adrenaline junkie to want to be in on any kind of trouble, especially if it threatened people in her domain. "Point them out to me," she whispered.

"They're over by the gift shop," Dorothy replied. She pointed and Kelly spotted them right away: three men, wearing long coats and dark clothing. Each man had a familiar look to them—these were criminals, all right, the sort of men that Kelly's husband spent far too much time in the company of. She saw Henry walking towards them but the men hadn't noticed him yet—they were staring at the children, watching as they laughed and played. The hair on the nape of Kelly's neck started to stand on end. She began walking towards them, unsure what was about to happen but knowing it wasn't going to be good. She didn't shout out because she wanted to avoid a panic and a part of her hoped that she was overreacting.

She saw Henry stop in front of the men and ask them something—and that was when it all went to hell. The closest of the men reached into his coat and pulled out a handgun—which he used to pistol whip Henry. The lovable security guard hit the floor and a little girl nearby saw what had happened and began screaming. Other children followed suit, especially when the other two men also brought out weapons.

Kelly couldn't fathom why these men were about to kill innocent children but she knew that was what was about to happen. Without regard for her own safety, she threw herself atop several of the nearest kids, blanketing them with her own body. She heard the pop-pop-pop of gunfire, the screams of the frightened and the injured and she knew that nothing would ever be the same for her or the museum ever again.

KELLY WASN'T SURE how long it lasted—even after the shooting stopped, the screaming continued. The children under her were sobbing so loudly and she'd continually whispered that it would all be okay, even as she shuddered in terror.

When she finally lifted her head and looked around, she saw so many children and adults on the floor, blood everywhere. The three gunmen were all dead of self-inflicted head shots.

Rising unsteadily, Kelly moved towards her office. She saw Dorothy poking her head out of the door, shaken but unharmed. "Have you called the police?" she asked her secretary.

"No," Dorothy stammered. "I was under the desk. I was too scared…"

"It's okay," Kelly said, embracing her friend for a moment before pulling away. "Go check on Henry while I get us some help."

Dorothy nodded, wiped her eyes, and left the office. Kelly took several deep breaths and then grabbed the phone. She didn't bother calling the police just yet—instead she dialed the phone number for 6196 Robeson Avenue. Even if Lazarus was out, there would be someone there to receive the message and relay it to him.

THE SHOCK AND horror had not abated the next day. The museum was closed and the newspapers were filled with stories about the terrible events and the impact it would have on the community. No one had ever heard of an event like this before and Kelly hoped it would be a one-time thing and not a harbinger of things to come.

She was at home, having elected to close the museum for the rest of the week. Standing in front of a window overlooking Robeson Avenue, she had her arms wrapped tightly about herself and she shivered, not from the cold but from the memory of what had happened. A heavy rain was falling outside and the building occasionally shook from powerful thunder. It was like God himself was crying and raging against the wrongness of what had happened.

She heard the door to the bedroom open and her acute sense of smell recognized the scent of her husband's aftershave. "I still can't believe it," she said. "All those children dead…just because that Woland character wanted to perform some sort of spell?"

Lazarus came up behind her and put his hands on her shoulders, gently massaging them. "The bullets the gunmen used were forged from the thirty pieces of silver. They killed the children because they were innocent."

"And did it work?"

"Woland seems to think so…and Abby says she's felt something strange in the air, like the calm before the storm."

Kelly turned to face her husband, her face looking pale. "You know I believe in what you're doing at Tartarus but in this case, I can't help but want to see him dead instead of sitting in a cell."

"I know…believe me, there's been plenty of times when I've felt the same about a lot of the people we lock up in Tartarus. What concerns me is the fact that he didn't put up a fight when we took him in." Lazarus let his head lean forward so his chin rested atop his wife's head. She slipped her arms around him and they held each other close. "He says it's too late…that he's gotten what he wanted. He doesn't want to escape because he says he wants to watch me as Sovereign City falls to pieces."

"Nothing's happened since the massacre," Kelly pointed out. "I mean, people are walking around in shock and the mayor's ordered all the flags to fly at half-mast but Woland's got to have more up his sleeve than that."

"He claims that the dead will begin walking the earth," Lazarus replied.

Kelly pulled away, looking concerned. "Any signs of that?"

"Not that I've heard—but Abby and Samantha have headed out to the city cemetery to look, just in case."

"Yuck...that place is creepy enough, without Woland's witchcraft to worry about."

Lazarus knew exactly what Kelly was talking about—she'd grown up in Sovereign, so the stories about the cemetery were deeply ingrained in her memory. The place was perpetually surrounded by a strange pink-tinged mist that clung to visitors' ankles. Local legend said that the mist was caused by all the evil of those buried there, seeping up through the ground. It was true that many of the more respectable families buried their dead in private graveyards rather than the city-owned one and so most of the new burials consisted of the poor, the unknown, or those that had been put to death by Sovereign City's famous Doc Daye.

"I'm glad you weren't hurt," he said and Kelly answered him with a shrug.

"I would have taken all those bullets myself if it would have saved even one of those children. My god, can you imagine what their parents are going through? What if Zeke had been there? Or Emily[6]?"

"They weren't," Lazarus said. "But I'll handle this like they had been...Woland will be punished for his role in this, I promise you."

"What if he really is the devil?" Kelly answered. "We don't have the first clue who those gunmen were, do we? We don't know where he got them from or how he convinced them to kill themselves. How are you going to stop him from snapping his fingers and vanishing to hell? Can you really stop him if he's Lucifer?"

---

6 Emily is Samantha's daughter—the product of a bizarre supernatural spell cast by Lazarus Gray's enemy, Nemesis.

"He may be a powerful sorcerer—he may even be a demon—but he's not the Devil himself. I've fought people that may fit that description but I don't think it's Woland. Even if he is what he says and he does escape, we'll just track him down again."

Kelly nodded but both of them were distracted when the building's intercom system came to life and Morgan's voice came through. "Lazarus?"

"I'm here, Morgan. What do you need?"

"Come downstairs, please—we've got visitors…from Berlin."

———

THE CEMETERY WAS quiet and the air seemed to drop several degrees in temperature as soon as Samantha and Abby stepped through the gates. Both of them carried umbrellas and wore slacks and flat-heeled shoes on account of the weather and the resulting muddy ground. The infamous pink-tinged mist did not drift past the gates—it hung right on the other side like a hungry dog denied permission to escape its master's yard.

"I don't like this," Samantha said, raising her voice to be heard over the pattering of rain on her umbrella.

"What do you mean?" Abby asked, carefully moving through the mist. It obscured her vision enough that she was worried about stepping into a hole—or even an open grave.

"The caretaker didn't answer our call…the gates are standing wide open even though the cemetery doesn't open to the public for another half hour. It's just strange, that's all."

"Don't let the setting get to you."

Samantha frowned, deciding she would keep the rest of her thoughts to herself. It wasn't simply that being in a cemetery was creepy—though it was, to be honest. There was more to it than that. The whole way that Woland had calmly walked into his cell and taken a seat on his cot, that pleased smile on his face…it was like he really had won. Were all his stories about the barriers between life and death falling apart true? What would that mean…?

A bit of movement caught Samantha's attention from the edge of her peripheral vision and she turned in that direction, expecting to see Dick Black, the caretaker. The man she locked eyes with was not Mr. Black, however—it was someone that quite literally took her breath away. She was barely able to gasp out, "Abby!"

When the witch stopped and looked to her right, her eyes widened in horror.

Lurching towards her was a dead man…his skin was rotted away in places, revealing white bone and gristle. His hair was nothing more than thin wisps that were plastered to his skull by the rain and his suit was moth-eaten and hung loosely off his emaciated frame. When he saw them, he raised one bony arm towards them, his fingers opening and closing on the air.

Samantha reacted with impressive speed—she lowered her umbrella, pointing the ferrule at the shambling figure. She squeezed on the handle and the umbrella discharged several bullets, each of which struck the walking corpse in the chest.

The figure staggered but continued on and Abby hissed, "You can't hurt him with bullets—not even silver-tipped ones!" The witch tossed aside her own umbrella and raised both hands, which began to glow with a swirling blue-and-white energy. She allowed this to exit her body in a powerful burst that struck the undead figure and caused it to literally explode.

Samantha's umbrella came back up and she grimaced as several fingers and part of the man's skull bounced off the protective covering. "Okay…so one dead person has risen. The question is: is he the first?"

"I don't think he is." Abby was ignoring the rain that was falling on her, choosing instead to move her hands slowly over the mist. It parted for her as she walked forward and Samantha saw many disturbed graves: the earth looked as if it had been shoved up from below and some of the tombstones lay on their sides. Here and there on the ground were more of the undead—some of them were no longer able to stand upright due to the effects of decomposition. Further out towards the center of the cemetery was a large group of undead—they were mingling about, bumping into one another. Some of them appeared to be trying to communicate but death was not kind to certain soft tissues in the mouth and throat so the most they could do was grunt or moan.

One of the undead emitted a different sort of noise and pointed at the two women, causing the entire group to suddenly start moving in a large pack towards them.

"I think we've found out what we need to know," Samantha whispered. "Shall we head back to the car?"

Before Abby could respond, the crack of a rifle made both women jump. One of the undead fell over, its head having suddenly split like an overripe melon.

Dick Black came running through the mist, rifle in hand, towards the gate—and by reason of proximity, the two heroes from Assistance Unlimited. He looked disheveled and his forehead was streaked with blood. "Get out! Get out!" he shouted. "The dead are walkin'! Can't ya see?" He paused just long enough to squeeze off another shot, this one missing the horde of dead entirely.

Abby knelt and snatched up her umbrella and she exited the graveyard with Samantha and Mr. Black. The caretaker swung the gates closed and locked them with a heavy chain.

Looking at the ladies, he gasped out his story. "I was walking the grounds this morning, checking things before we started the day—and one of those *things* started digging its way outta the grave! Scared me so bad I nearly wet myself and I fell in that hole they dug for Mrs. Scoggins…she's supposed to be buried this afternoon but that sure as hell ain't happenin'! Forgive my language."

"You're forgiven," Samantha said. "Get in the car, Mr. Black—we'll drop you off at home on our way to Robeson Avenue."

"I'm staying here," Abby said. She tossed the keys to Samantha, who caught them by the keychain. "Those things are going to try to get through the gates—one or two of them wouldn't stand a chance but the whole graveyard? They just might get through. I'll hold them off until Lazarus decides what to do—but he needs to know that this might be happening at all the graveyards in the city!"

Samantha nodded and grabbed hold of Mr. Black's sleeve. "Don't get hurt, Abby!"

"I'll try not to," the witch replied. She smelled the stench of death approaching and she swallowed hard, watching as the risen corpses of Sovereign shambled towards her.

The car pulled out with squealing tires behind her but Abby remained firmly where she was, her hands glowing once more. She would not allow these creatures to get past her—if need be, she would blow up this entire field, taking her own life in the process.

CHAPTER X
RISING PASSIONS

CHARLES "CHUCK" DIXON took another bite of his cruller, not caring that bits of food were clinging to his bushy moustache. He wore gloves and an apron over his white shirt and dark pants, his customary attire when working in the city morgue.

Most days he dealt with drunks or the bullet-riddled bodies of gangsters...today things were a little bit rougher given that he was dealing with the corpses of a couple dozen children. It wasn't so much that he hated the idea of cutting them open—his professional walls were so intact that he was never bothered by that sort of thing. No, it was the confrontation with a set of angry parents about an hour ago that had soured his mood. They were adamant that there be no autopsy carried out...they wanted their precious babies left "intact," as if they didn't have holes all over their bodies from the bullets. Dixon had tried to explain that this was a major crime and he owed it to his superiors to give them answers. Yes, everybody knew how they had died but there might still be questions that could be answered by his work. He had sworn that the kids would look perfect when the time came for the funerals.

The last of the cruller disappeared into his mouth and he washed it down with the remnants of some lukewarm coffee. It was time to get to work—he'd filled out all the paperwork he could without actually getting his hands dirty.

He picked up a scalpel and turned to the first body that he'd prepared for the day—a nine year old girl named Suzanne Rothstein. She was a cute little thing, or would have been when she was alive. You wouldn't have been able to tell that she was Jewish if you hadn't heard her last name, either—Dixon couldn't stand the Jews with the huge noses. It was just a personal preference, he supposed.

Just before he turned around, he heard a rustling of fabric. He paused, knowing that he was alone in the room…but then why was he hearing so much *movement*?

He turned slowly and his mouth fell open in shock. The dead children…they were sitting up, some were looking right at him, one of them—Suzanne—had even swung her legs off the examining table and was tentatively trying to stand. She swayed on unsteady legs, like she couldn't remember how they were supposed to work.

Dixon took several steps back, stopping only when his behind touched the cold brick wall. The dead were coming for him with slack mouths, outstretched hands and eyes that were as empty as their souls.

The little Jew girl reached him first, her thin lips peeling back to reveal a set of perfectly white teeth. Suzanne jumped up on him, her legs wrapping about his waist and right when Dixon's mind broke out of its shocked state and he realized he needed to fight or scream or *do something*, it was too late. The girl's mouth clamped around his throat and suddenly she was chewing into his flesh…

Dixon's words were lost in a gurgle of flowing blood.

ALF REACHED UP and slowly undid the buckles that held his mask in place. Once it was off, he set it aside and ran a gloved hand through his hair. He'd grown accustomed to breathing with the mask in place but it still made his face sweat. "I had to call in some favors to get out of the country," he said, turning to face Lazarus and Eun, who were seated around Assistance Unlimited's briefing room table. "Nakam's saved a few people that still have enough pull to get Karl and I safe passage."

"Won't this Captain Krieger character discover that you've gone missing?" Eun asked.

"Possibly—depends on how long I'm gone. I did leave word with my landlord that I would be away on business. Hopefully Krieger will assume that I'm still looking for Karl." Alf sat down and looked at Lazarus. As usual, the leader of Assistance Unlimited was a stoic figure and it was difficult for Alf to read the man's thoughts. "So these Crimson Ladies that I fought…it matches up with what this Woland character told you?"

"Yes," Lazarus responded. "I feel rather bad for you, though—all this you've been doing to find Karl…I'm not sure if it really has any value. The information you gathered was given to us by Woland and Karl was not meant to be anything other than a red herring for everyone to chase and waste time."

Alf shrugged. "Perhaps…or maybe there's more at work here than just Woland. If there's a devil, then surely that means there's someone on the other side, right? I like to think that they might have been trying to make sure that I ended up here so that I could help."

Eun chuckled. He liked Alf—the man was brave as hell to do what he did right in the serpent's lair—but he also knew that what he'd just said revealed a good bit of ego. The notion that God was bringing Nakam to Sovereign was pretty self-inflated.

"Well, you are here now," Lazarus said, "and you're right in that we could certainly use you. I've sent a couple of agents out to check on the supposed 'rising of the dead' and--"

Morgan's voice over the intercom interrupted them. "Lazarus, I just got a call from Samantha. She's dropping off Mr. Black from the cemetery but she says there's something awful going on at the graveyard. Looks like Woland was telling the truth. Abby's back there on her own, holding off the hordes."

Lazarus stood quickly, replying, "Morgan, tell Bob to stay here with The Puzzler and his cousin…I want everyone else to meet me out front." To Alf, he asked, "You're with us?"

"You couldn't hold me back."

"Good. Morgan, you still listening?"

"Loud and clear, Chief," Morgan said.

"Call the Mayor and give him the basic situation. Tell him we're on the case but he might want to see if Fortune McCall or Doc Daye are in town. I suspect we're going to need all hands on deck."

———⚬⚭⚬———

BOB BENTON, WEARING his Black Terror costume but having exchanged the domino mask for a pair of glasses, entered the room that had been set aside for The Puzzler, letting the door fall shut behind him a little bit harder than he'd intended. The occupants, Ronald and Karl, looked up in surprise from where they were seated on the bed. Something in their expressions looked guilty and Bob felt the color rise to his cheeks—he'd begun to suspect that The Puzzler's "friendship" with his cousin went beyond the norm.

The Puzzler grinned, unable to keep from twisting the proverbial blade in his longtime enemy. "Must gall you to be left behind to babysit us. You'd think they'd want the team's strongman with them. I mean, they seriously took that old man—Morgan—with them and didn't take *you*?"

Bob felt his anger rise but he bit it down, not wanting to take the bait. "Everyone takes turns manning the homefront. Besides, nobody else has as much experience as I do when it comes to you."

"Oh, so I suppose I should be flattered, then? They think I'm such a threat to escape unless my arch-nemesis is here to stop me." The Puzzler turned to look at his cousin and his voice seemed to soften as he said, "Does all this seem silly to you?"

Karl looked at Ronald's costume and then over at Bob's. "To be honest? A bit. At least Nakam is just wearing a mask and a suit—all of this is a bit flamboyant." A crooked smile appeared on Karl's lips. "Even for you."

Bob sat down in a chair nearby and picked up the newspaper that The Puzzler had been looking at earlier. He flipped to the comic strips and saw that the villain had completed the crossword, the word jumble and the daily riddles. He lowered the paper just enough to see that the two men on the bed were leaning close to one another, whispering. It was strange to see The Puzzler like this…normally when Bob was around the man, it was a matter of physical conflict. He wasn't used to viewing Ronald as a human being, with friendships and love affairs. Frowning, he reminded himself that Ronald was a killer—just because he might have a softer side didn't mean he wasn't dangerous or that he didn't deserve to spend the rest of his life in prison.

With a sigh, Bob closed the paper and tossed it aside. He stood up and said, "Look, I get the feeling you two want to catch up. If I leave you alone for a little while, do you give me your word that you won't try to escape?"

The Puzzler laughed. "*Try* to escape? Certainly not! If I try, I'll succeed."

Karl frowned and held a hand over his cousin's mouth to silence him. "Ignore him. You have my word."

The Black Terror studied the thin, sunken-eyed German and finally nodded. "Okay. I'll be just down the hall, keeping track of the others via the short-wave radio. You guys…be good."

Without waiting to see if The Puzzler gave a snide reply, Bob exited the room. He stood on the other side of the door for a minute and then shook his head. He wasn't sure he could trust his old enemy but maybe this Karl character would be a good influence on him.

He certainly can't make him any worse, he mused.

CHAPTER XI
A CITY IN TURMOIL

MORTIMER QUINN PACED back and forth behind his office desk, hating that his life now consisted of fielding phone calls and sending others into harm's way.

Once upon a time, the man that was currently Sovereign City's mayor had been the servant of The Voice, a mystical figure that had empowered him to battle the forces of darkness as one of his Gravediggers. He had served his time in this role, vanquishing evil again and again. Since then he'd wandered the world, aging far slower than most. When he'd come to Sovereign to investigate the first woman to wield the mantle of Gravedigger[7], he'd fallen in love with the city and decided to stay. After falsifying a background for himself to hide his true age, Mortimer had run for mayor and won…now he continued to try and wage the good fight, though he no longer did so with his fists and or with a sword.

Jean Starr, his steadfast secretary, poked her head into his office. "Sir? The police chief just called—it's like you said: there are reports of dead people walking around all over the city. But it's not just the people…there are reports of animals, too."

Mortimer sighed and turned to face her. "Come in and have a seat."

Jean cast a glance back to her own desk, where the phone was ringing again. It had been going non-stop since she'd gotten to the office.

"Just leave it," Mortimer said, "We both know what they're calling about and there's not a whole lot we can do about it."

---

7 Charity Grace, the star of The Adventures of Gravedigger trilogy.

When Jean reluctantly sat down, Mortimer perched himself on the edge of his desk. He rubbed his hands together in front of him and looked at her with a steady gaze. The two of them had confided in each other not long after meeting one another, each sensing a kindred spirit. Thus, she knew of his past as Gravedigger and he was aware of her relationship with Bob Benton, aka The Black Terror.

"I talked to Charity a little while ago," he said. "She and her team are out hitting up some of the smaller graveyards on the outskirts of town—if we can stop those things from making it into the city proper, all the better. I've got a meeting with the religious leaders in an hour, too, so you need to put that on the schedule and clear out the conference room."

"I will," Jean replied. "Tim just stopped by—he's going to try and help out around the city, too. I told him that Bob was manning the home office for Assistance Unlimited but he said there was no way he was going over to sit around—'twiddling his thumbs' is how he put it."

"One half of the Terror Twins is better than nothing," Mortimer said. He paused and then added, "Are you religious?"

"No, not really," she admitted. "You?"

"After being resurrected from the dead by a disembodied voice that threatened me with eternal damnation if I didn't do its bidding? Yes, I am." He reached out a hand and after she took it, he asked, "Will you pray with me?"

Jean smiled and nodded. "Of course."

Both of them lowered their heads and Mortimer began his prayers, saying, "Even though I walk through the valley of the shadow of death, I fear no evil; for Thou art with me; Thy rod and Thy staff, they comfort me…"

"JESUS CHRIST…"

Morgan pulled the roadster over to the side of the road, stopping a little ways away from the gate into the cemetery. The ground was on fire—a mystical blue flame burned so brightly that Morgan had to avert his gaze.

Just outside the gates was Abby, standing atop a mound of dead bodies, some of them still twitching. She looked like a figure straight out of a trashy pulp magazine: her clothing was ripped, revealing more of her figure than was meant to be bared in public; her hair was flowing in a stiff breeze; her eyes and hands were crackling with magic fire; and her lips were pulled back in an expression of pure fury. As Morgan exited the vehicle, joined by his friends, he stared open-mouthed as Abby raised her hands and fired another burst of energy—this one struck an old oak tree, causing it to split down the middle of its mighty form. It toppled over onto a group of undead.

Morgan glanced over at Lazarus and asked, "So…*we're* here to help *her?*"

TIM ROLAND HATED it when people called him Black Terror Jr. but he did admit that it was better than when his mentor called him "Tim" when he was in costume. Talk about not knowing how to protect a secret identity…

The city was a mess—cars had crashed on the sides of the street as drivers swerved to hit the walking dead that shambled down the center of the road. The reanimated corpses seemed uniformly aggressive, killing all those they can into contact with…and those dead would then rise, as well, joining the growing hordes.

Sprinting through the fires and trying to filter out the screams so that he could focus on the people in immediate danger, Tim crossed into a small subdivision not far from the town square. He heard a little girl's cries and he turned, cocking his head to try and zero in on where she was—he spotted her in a tree nearby, her legs drawn up under her hanging skirt. She looked no more than seven years old and tears were running off her chubby cheeks.

At the base of the tree, standing on its hind legs and emitting strange, guttural barks, was a resurrected puppy—its ribs showing through its matted fur, poking through desiccated skin. One of its ears hung by a tiny strip of flesh and its muzzle had mostly rotted away, revealing the sharp teeth in its mouth. Its eyes were glassy, just like the other dead that Tim had seen—but somehow it was able to focus on its prey, as if drawn to the very life that it no longer possessed.

"Hey, scruffy!" Tim yelled. The demonic puppy dropped back to all fours and turned towards The Black Terror's young partner. It growled deep in its throat and began to move towards the hero...like the reanimated humans, it moved in a herky-jerky fashion, as if its limbs no longer remembered how they should function.

Tim was fairly certain that the beast's claws and teeth couldn't pierce his hardened skin, which was almost as dense as his mentor's...but he was in no hurry to test that. Besides, for all he knew, these monsters had some sort of poison in them that could kill just through contact!

As the canine neared him, Tim leaped over the creature. He landed in a crouch behind the beast and he seized the back of its neck with both hands, lifting it off the ground. He loved animals but he didn't feel any remorse for what he did next—the rigidity of the body, the smell of decay and the strange sounds that it emitted all worked to remind him that this was no ordinary dog...this was a monster.

Pulling with all his superhuman strength, Tim felt the dog's skin and tissue stretch before giving way. The puppy's head was yanked free from the rest of its body and Tim tossed it away. Remarkably, its mouth still opened and closed, its teeth snapping on the empty air. Disgusted, Tim moved towards the head and stomped it repeatedly until it was a mess beneath his boot and the dog's mouth no longer worked.

Turning back to the girl, Tim was prepared to tell her it was safe and he could escort her back home...but she was gone, having scrambled out of the tree and run away during his confrontation with the dog. He couldn't really blame her but he hoped that she would be safe...

Looking down at his leg, he saw that it was covered with gore. Shivering a bit, he scrubbed the bottom of his boot on the road's asphalt surface. After taking several deep breaths, he resumed his slow trek through the city, looking for more people to save.

A streaking object in the sky caught his attention and Tim looked up just in time to see the mysterious silver-and-blue figure of the man called Babylon[8] pass overhead. Bob had told him that the Negro sometimes referred to himself as the "cosmic force of retribution," whatever that meant. Tim hoped that the flying man could make a difference out here—because right now it certainly felt like the beginning of The End.

———∞∞∞———

ASSISTANCE UNLIMITED HAD split up after ensuring that the Sovereign City Cemetery was no longer posing a threat. Lazarus had asked Morgan, Samantha, and Eun to take the car and continue patrolling the city—there were many people out there that needed help and the local authorities were proving ill-equipped to deal with the psychological ramifications of facing the risen dead.

Meanwhile, Abby, Lazarus, and Nakam had journeyed to Tartarus to speak with Woland. On the way over Lazarus had asked Abby to warn Nakam about what she'd seen in her vision: that he would be gunned down with the very same silver bullets that had been used to kill those children. Nakam had accepted the warnings stoically, merely nodding and saying nothing in response.

The trio entered the prison and Lazarus noted that Nakam seemed somewhat disturbed by what he saw—he doubted that it was the obscenities that some of the men screamed at them as they went past but he wasn't certain.

"Something wrong?" he whispered.

Nakam's reply came after a moment's consideration. "I'm just surprised that you're able to do this… I thought your justice system made allowances for a fair trial and an assumption of innocence."

"You're right—I'm sure I'm violating quite a few civil liberties. The authorities turn a blind eye in some cases and in others they actually

---

8 Babylon has worked with Assistance Unlimited in the past, as well as starring in The Second Book of Babylon.

aid me in keeping this place running. They don't have the facilities to house most of these men and women—and the few people in power that actually place a value on justice know that it's better to have these criminals housed here than in a traditional prison anyway. There's no graft to be had here...no underhanded deals being made. Men like Professor Thorne over there," Lazarus pointed towards a handsome man doing exercises in his cell, "He'd outwit an ordinary security system in no time. He's adept at not just human psychology but also the supernatural. Putting him in a maximum-security cell at the state pen isn't going to stop him for more than a couple of days. The mayor is an old friend and has experience with the more...unusual...types of crime so he's a bit more understanding than some others might be."

"What about on a Federal level, though? You can't have kept this a secret from the United States government..."

"We have a working agreement with an organization known as Project: Cicada. Our liaison helps us stay in the clear of any Federal intervention." Lazarus glanced at Nakam as they turned down a hallway that held only one cell—it was located at a dead-end and was lit by a single yellow bulb that swayed a bit as the wall-mounted air-conditioning unit ran at full blast. Abby had long ago decided that it was better to let each prisoner control their own thermostats since no two of them could agree on whether it was too hot or too cold. Lazarus spoke quietly to Nakam, "If you have some sort of moral problem with Tartarus, you're welcome to get a full tour and see that we treat them better than they deserve."

"No—and I'm sorry if I came off as thinking that way. A prison where no jury sentences you and there's no systematic way of possibly earning your freedom... Well, it sounds a lot like some of the things we have back home right now. Not that I'm comparing you to our Fuehrer, of course."

Abigail stopped in front of Woland's cell and the men that had been trailing along behind came to a halt on either side of her. Woland, who appeared to her now as an overweight man in his late thirties, with an olive-complexion, oily hair and a small scar on his double chin, looked up from his cot and smiled. His upper right canine was adorned by a small diamond that had been set into the enamel. "Mr. Woland," she said. "We'd like to talk to you."

"I was wondering when you would come see me," Woland said. "My accommodations are not the best for hosting visitors but you're free to come in if you like."

"We'll stay out here," Abby replied. "The dead are rising from their graves, just like you said."

Woland gestured to her bloodstained clothes and nodded. "I see you've made their acquaintance."

"Why are they all so evil?" Nakam asked. "Spirits tried to warn Lazarus and Morgan earlier—shouldn't some of these risen dead be more like they were in life?"

"Returning from the afterlife is not an easy experience," Woland said without hesitation. "It's one thing for a spirit, a wraith, to appear to someone. It's another for that same spirit to suddenly be trapped inside a rotting corpse of a shell. Can you imagine? To be inside a body that was once your own but is now literally falling apart? To be aware of your own decomposition? To see the horror in the eyes of the living and know that you are the one causing it? It's no wonder that almost all of them are driven insane by their resurrection. They are then driven to slay the living for they suddenly embody all that the dead are not."

"How do we reverse it?" Lazarus asked.

"Why would I tell you how to do that?" Woland asked with a laugh. "It's partially yourself that's to blame... I think having all your chickens coming home to roost is quite fitting." With a limp, the man moved to his cot and sat back down. "Besides, I'm tired of ruling in the Underworld. Let Hell come to earth—I'll take my time sitting on my sunlit throne."

"Because if you don't, I'll destroy you," Lazarus replied. He drew his .357 Smith & Wesson Magnum and pointed it through the bars of Woland's cell. "Want to take a guess about what kind of bullets are in this gun?"

Woland stared at Lazarus, eyes narrowing. "You wouldn't dare..."

"Why not? It's a better use for them than killing children, wouldn't you say? And they're just crackling with mystical energy right now," Lazarus said. "Want to see how badly they could hurt you?"

Woland shrugged but all three of them could see the fury in his expression. For a supposed "Lord of Lies," he was not proving to be very good at hiding his emotions. "Go ahead. Even if you slay this body, I'll return. I am the Devil...and you cannot kill me, not even with those bullets."

"Maybe if you really were the Devil, that might be true," Lazarus said. "But we both know that's not who you are. I've been looking into references to you...and Abby's done some scrying. We already suspected you were bragging too much to be who you claimed, and I think we've been able to prove it. You know so much about the Thirty Pieces of Silver because you were there, weren't you? Your name has been lost to the annals of time but you've been called Ahasver, Matathias, Buttadeus, Paul, Isaac, Joseph...and Woland. The title most people know you by is The Wandering Jew."

Nakam's head jerked as he heard this—no one had bothered to tell him these facts on the way over. The Wandering Jew was, according to the New Testament, a Jew that had taunted Jesus on the way to the crucifixion. A curse was put upon the man, condemning him to walk the earth until the second coming of Christ. Nakam knew that stories conflicted not only on the man's name but also his appearance and his vocation—some said he had been a shoemaker, some said he was the doorman at Pontius Pilate's estate. Perhaps those variations were in some related to the way that everyone saw Woland differently...

Lazarus pulled back the hammer on his gun and said, "So I think you're right that these bullets won't *kill* you but I bet they'll hurt an awful lot...and none of the stories I've come across say you heal any faster than a normal man, you just don't die. Isn't that right?"

Woland let out a long, weary sigh. When he spoke, his voice carried with it both a sense of resignation and of utter disgust. "I do hate you, Lazarus Gray...do you know why? It's not because you've weakened the barriers, like I kept saying. That was just an excuse. A lie. No, I hate you because you destroyed the only group of men that I ever considered my equals. The Illuminati. I was a founding member of their organization, coming and going under numerous identities over the years. When you tore them down, I swore that someday I'd get my revenge upon you... and if I could somehow help usher in the final days of humanity, all the better! I've seen it all. I know the hypocrisy of man and the horrible truth that lies beneath all of our civilized veneer. We're all sinners, we're all beasts, we're all monsters!" Woland's voice had risen now and specks of phlegm flew from his mouth with every shouted utterance. "The Silver Coins were meant to help bring you down, to plunge the world into its proper Hellish punishment and..." His voice suddenly dropped and he turned away, leaving his words unfinished.

"And you wanted to draw out Lilith," Abby said, nodding with absolute certainty. "You know her...don't you?"

"We were lovers, long ago," Woland admitted. "She'll come for those bullets and she'll see me again, whether she wants to or not. She's hidden from me for ages, refused to answer any of my summons...but I know that her obsession with those coins will bring her out into the light."

Lazarus shook his head in disbelief. "All this. At its core, it's not really about me or about your hatred of the world. You're a scorned lover looking to reconnect with a woman that's spurned you."

"Don't belittle me," Woland whispered. "Our love was an epic one...but I made a mistake. I didn't think it was a very large one but she considered it the final straw. She cast me out—just like God had thrown her out of Eden."

"Tell me how to fight this," Lazarus continued, "and I give you my word that I'll make sure you see Lilith again."

"I'll even speak to her on your behalf," Abby said. "Sometimes hearing from another woman that a man's changed can make all the difference."

Sensing that this line of reasoning was having its intended effect, Nakam jumped in the fray, adding, "It's probably hard for her to find men that can be her equal—she's an immortal, after all. I imagine she's just as lonely as you are. If she's anything like the women I've known, it's partially a matter of pride keeping her from forgiving you. Women don't like to see themselves as weak—especially not a woman like her—and taking you back would be admitting vulnerability."

Abby nodded approvingly at Nakam and the trio settled in to wait, hoping that Woland would be swayed by their arguments.

After a moment's pause, Woland nodded. "I'll tell you, Lazarus Gray…because I think all you'll end up doing is getting yourself killed." He smiled broadly. "So by all means, get busy! Here's what you need to do…"

CHAPTER XII
MOTHER OF MONSTERS

THE ZEPPELIN PASSED through the clouds, momentarily becoming silhouetted against the full moon that hung bloated and round above Sovereign City. The famed metropolis had begun evacuating residents in the mid-afternoon but many refused to leave—Sovereign citizens prided themselves on their refusal to bow down before the strange or bizarre. Indeed, bands of vigilantes had organized themselves long before the evacuation order came. They moved through the city, shooting the undead in the head or hacking them to pieces with homemade implements of war.

Onboard the unmarked zeppelin, a crew of nearly two dozen women manned the controls. Each of them was cloaked from head to toe in scarlet robes. Their hoods were thrown back since they were in the privacy of their sisters, revealing a wide range of ages and ethnicities. The Crimson Ladies did not discriminate in any way besides gender… they viewed men as the lesser sex, too easily swayed by their sexual urges.

The captain of the vessel, a tall, statuesque African by the name of Arjana, walked up a series of steps that led to a private passenger room. The sliding door that restricted access was open, revealing the ship's special guest: the leader and founder of the Crimson Ladies, the so-called Mother of Monsters…Lilith.

Arjana paused inside the door, standing erect with her hands clasped behind her back. The Nubian beauty loved her mistress, as did all members of the organization. Lilith embodied so much for them: the strength that all women possessed but that few men wanted to recognize;

the ability to recover from the loss of a relationship; and the kind of simmering fury that only a female could truly nurse.

Lilith sat in a large chair, her body curled so that her legs hung over one arm. She was slinky like a cat, her body able to achieve an amazing dichotomy: she was both lithe and yet full-figured, slim and yet curvaceous. Her dark hair was lustrous, hanging past her shoulders in delicate curls…and her lips were somewhat cruel in shape, matching the callous cynicism visible in her eyes. She wore a cream-colored sweater fringed with sable fur, a white leather belt cinched tight and khaki pants. Her leather boots came up just past her ankle and one foot bobbed up and down in time, like a cat's tail swishing side to side. The overall effect of her being was feline, right down to that potentially fatal stare— she looked like something that yearned to be touched but which had the potential to strike any who dared.

"Captain?" Lilith purred, her eyes narrowing to slits.

Arjana moved a few steps closer to Lilith's chair, keeping her rigid posture. "We have arrived, madam."

"And the state of the city?"

"As the news reports have suggested, a massive evacuation has begun but there are still many figures on the city streets. At this point, we can't be certain how many are alive…and how many are the resurrected."

Lilith swung her legs to the floor and rose, arching her back as she stretched. "I don't like that term for them…resurrection implies something wonderful. What's been done to these poor souls—it's not a miracle, it's a sin." She placed her hands on her hips and looked down at Arjana. They were normally of equal height but the heels on Lilith's boots put her a good three inches taller. "Tell me again what Gray said."

Arjana's face betrayed no emotion but the airship was awash with gossip. Though no woman onboard aside from Lilith herself remembered Woland's affair with their mistress, rumors had spread for years about a man obsessed with her—a former partner that had strayed once too often and been banished from her life. Until earlier today, Arjana had dismissed them all. She had never known Lilith to take a man to her bed…but after Lazarus Gray had sent a radio message to one of the

Crimson Ladies' listening posts in Brazil, there had been no doubt about the stories' veracity. Lilith had immediately taken her crew to flight, traveling at top speed to North America. "'Woland has unleashed a plague of the dead upon Sovereign City and it will spread to the rest of the world if left unchecked. I need your help, Lilith.'" She paused and then added, "That was it, just a repeating message. It could be a trap."

Lilith waved away the warning. "It's not. Gray is not our enemy… and it makes sense that the silver coins would be linked to Woland. He always did like to play dangerous games." She crossed her room to the luxurious bed she had brought onboard with her. It was nothing like the austere cots that the crew slept on though no one onboard begrudged her for such things. She had suffered like few women on earth—scorned by her husband, by the authors of the bible and, in the end, by God himself. If a few creature comforts could offer her pleasure, Arjana was more than willing to let her have them.

Lilith began picking through the suitcase that lay open atop the bed. She tossed aside a plethora of clothing of all colors and styles. She carried attire with her for any weather condition and for any potential social event—be it slumming in the streets of New Delhi or attending a political event in Washington, D.C. She had dozens of false identities, with papers that placed her nationality as American, English, German, Scandinavian, and even Egyptian.

At the bottom of the bag, she pulled out a sheath that contained a 14th-century Auray Rondel dagger. Lilith pulled the weapon from its sheath and moved it slightly, letting the light play along its blade. The guard was plated in 24-karat gold with elaborate filigree work on the pommel. The wooden handle was covered in black leather with a swirled gold chain. She had slain many foes with this weapon over the years and Arjana knew that she loved the blade with a passion she reserved for little else.

"Are the girls talking?" Lilith asked, casting a glance over her shoulder at Arjana.

Somehow finding a way to stiffen even more, Captain Arjana knew that telling a lie to her mistress was not a way to maintain her position. "There are…stories. It's difficult for some to picture you with a man."

"Everyone knows my past," Lilith pointed out. "I was with Adam… and then many others. How could I be the 'mother of monsters' if I'd never been with a man?" she asked laughingly.

"It's been…a while?"

Lilith grinned though the smile didn't touch her eyes. "Don't rub it in, Arjana…"

For a second Arjana feared that she'd insulted her mistress and she opened her mouth, readying an apology. When she saw Lilith fastening the sheath to the side of her belt, letting it rest against her hip, she realized that Lilith wasn't truly offended—or, if she was, she had no desire in punishing the airship captain. "There is a mooring mast atop the Tartarus prison facility. Though no dirigible has actually docked there, we should be able to use the apparatus to winch the ship to it— winds are calm at the moment so you should be able to travel down the gangplank with no problem."

"Good," Lilith replied. She turned to face the captain and said, "Tell the crew that I may be older than anyone can count…but I'm still a woman. Woland was my lover but he betrayed me and I haven't let any man play me for a fool since. I'm not going to change that now."

"No one thinks you'll take him back," Arjana said fervently.

"Good," Lilith said, a peculiar expression on her face. "But I figured you ladies would be more concerned about me losing my head over Lazarus Gray. *That's* a man that might make any woman give up a vow of celibacy!"

IT WAS NEAR dawn when Lilith's airship was finally successfully maneuvered onto the docking mooring. The gangplank was extended and fully connected to the roof of Tartarus—it gently swayed in the breeze but was held relatively firm.

Lilith strode down the ramp alone, having directed her crew to remain behind. The sable fur that lined her shirt fluttered a bit in the wind and she looked like she could have stepped right off a red carpet movie premiere... if it wasn't for the way her eyes swept over her surroundings with the practiced stare of a fighter.

Lazarus stood waiting for her beside an open door that revealed a flight of stairs leading down into the facility. He was even more handsome than she'd expected—tall, well-formed in all ways, with a piercing stare and a dimpled chin. Only a few months before, she had briefly met a young man serving as communications officer in anti-submarine warfare aboard the USS PC-1137 and the resemblance between the two of them was uncanny. What had been his name? Douglas...Kirk Douglas[9]. She remembered because he'd been so good-looking and some feminine intuition had told her that he had a bright future ahead of him.

Lazarus stepped forward and extended a hand. His voice was deep but strangely monotone. "Welcome to Tartarus."

Lilith shook with him, her eyes locking onto his. She found the mismatched colors—one an emerald green, the other a dull brown—rather enchanting. In many ways, she thought his eyes were like a good description of men in general—there was something obviously beautiful about them but there was the plainer, earthier truth alongside that. "Have you figured out how to return the dead to their graves?" she asked.

Lazarus began walking with her down the stairs. "Woland gave me some information. We're in the process of finishing up our preparations. Bringing you here was his payment for assisting us." Lazarus reached into a pocket and retrieved a small bag that he held out to her. Its contents clinked together with a metallic sound and Lilith's eyes opened wide.

"The thirty pieces of silver," she said quietly, gingerly taking the bag.

"They're bullets now."

Lilith stopped at the foot of the stairs, staring at the sack. "Why are you giving these to me? Do you have any idea of how dangerous they are...and how untrustworthy most people consider me?"

"Woland gave me a lot of detail about you and I spent most of last

9 Yes, *that* Kirk Douglas. One of the visual inspirations for Lazarus Gray, Douglas would make his feature film debut in 1946's *The Strange Love of Martha Ivers*.

night reading up on you. I don't believe you're a villain, no matter what the church had said about you. You're a willful woman…and that should never be a crime."

"Well, aren't you an open-minded man." Lilith held the sackful of bullets out to Lazarus. "Take them. I've done my diligence in trying to scatter them. It's your turn. I trust you." She winked at him and added, "I've done some reading about you, too."

Nodding, Lazarus led her past Abby's office. The door was open and Abigail spotted them, rising from her chair and crossing around her desk in a hurried attempt to catch up to them. She looked at Lilith with an expression that obviously seemed strange to Lazarus but which was one quickly recognized by Lilith—many young women regarded her with open admiration, like she was a movie star.

"Lilith!" Abby said, her breath coming in rapid gasps. When the other woman turned to look at her, the brunette warden said, "I'm a witch and I've always admired you…I even use your name in some of my incantations!"

"It's nice to meet you, sister." Lilith reached out and touched Abby on the arm. "Abigail Cross?"

"Yes!" Abby beamed, obviously pleased that Lilith knew her name.

"I'm glad to see that Lazarus has placed you in charge of this facility. It's another sign that he understands that our gender doesn't preclude us from handling dangerous jobs." Lilith lowered her voice, asking in an aside, "How are the rest of the men on the team? Are they as mature as your leader?"

"More or less," Abby replied. "Morgan's a little old-fashioned but you'll like him. He genuinely loves women."

"Then he's a rare one," Lilith said, her playful tone suddenly shifting to one of barely restrained anger. "Most men secretly hate us…they despise the way we are the gatekeepers of sexuality, our refusal to allow them to live a life of pure physicality and how we force them to deal with those uncomfortable emotions. That's why they want to subjugate us so badly."

Abby nodded in agreement but quickly added, "If you want another sign that Lazarus and the rest of the guys here aren't like that—they admitted they needed help from a woman. They don't mind doing that but they don't overuse it, either. They're not looking for a female to mother them and do their work for them."

"Good. I can tell you're happy here." Lilith turned back to Lazarus and said, "May I see Woland first? I'd like to get that out of the way and then you can tell me how I can help resolve this situation."

"Yes—but I would ask that you keep it as short as possible," Lazarus said. "The situation here in Sovereign is somewhat stable but everyone new that dies is then revived as one of these…things. Doc Daye and others are doing all they can to help out but the dead vastly outnumber the living after the evacuation. And we're seeing the effects beginning to spread to nearby counties and cities."

"I don't think it'll take long," she said. She placed a hand atop her dagger's handle and added, "Not long at all."

WOLAND BRIGHTENED WHEN he saw the cell door swing open and Lilith stepped within. Unlike virtually every other person on earth, she saw him as he truly was…there was no artifice to hide his true nature and she did not shrink away from it.

As opposed to Lilith, who remained perpetually young and beautiful, Woland aged…though he could not die. His body was withered and stooped, with skin so tight that you could see the outline of every bone. He looked like a living mummy, with thin wisps of hair on a liver spotted scalp. Everything about him spoke of antiquity, from the out-of-fashion Victorian-era suit he wore to the sunken sockets containing his beady eyes.

"Lilith," he said, allowing each syllable to slide across his lips like honey. "You are still so beautiful."

She glanced around the cell before speaking. Her own tone was carefully neutral—he might have described it as "cold" though he also knew that she could have been much frostier. He'd seen it—and experienced it. "Woland. I know you've been whining about missing me for a few centuries now and I have to tell you—it's not an attractive look. It might flatter a girl for a decade or two but after a while it just makes you look craven."

"I am sorry…"

"Yes, you've told me that again and again." Lilith looked at him sharply when he approached, dragging his lame left foot behind him. "Don't even think about touching me," she warned.

Woland looked down, pain evident in his face…but when he glanced up, he was wearing a shield of indignant anger. Like most men, he was all too ready to lean into anger rather than face emotional pain. "You're still a bitch."

"Bitch is just a man's preferred word for a woman that won't drop to her knees and kiss his feet." Before Woland could reply, she said, "Let's not drag this out—I'm here to help Lazarus end this nonsense. He said it was part of your deal with him that I speak with you. That's the only reason I'm in this filthy cell with you. I don't want to ever see you again. Do you finally understand that?"

Woland's anger was almost palpable and she could see that his hands were shaking…but there was no softening in her heart. Once she had made the final decision to end a relationship, it was over and done. She would never again take that man into her heart.

"You can't help him," Woland said last.

"You can't tell me what to do."

"I'm not trying to control you, woman! Gray is going to die on this fool's errand! It's impossible. Even with all of his knowledge and his friends, he's going to fail. If you go with him…you'll die, too."

Lilith sighed. "You're an awful man, Woland…but I have to admit, the fact that you're still worried about me is almost sweet." When he looked up suddenly, hope flaring in his eyes, she cut him off with a slice of her hand through the air and a stern warning. "It's not *that* sweet! I'm going to help him because it's the right thing to do—and as much as I often hate mankind, it's still worth saving. The fact that you've killed so many just to try and lure me back to you…it shows that you've never learned your lesson. Not after what you did to Christ, not after playing God with the Illuminati and not after losing me. You're just as much of an idiot now as you ever were!"

Woland reached out to the wall to stabilize himself. When he spoke, his eyes were closed and she could see just how tired he truly was. "Then kill me, Lilith. Please. You know as well as I that only God—or someone nearly as old as the earth itself—can do it. I'm weary. There's no hope for me to redeem myself. Please. Just take your knife…and end me."

For a long moment, Lilith stood there with her hand on the hilt of her blade. She wavered in her decision but in the end, she spun on her heels and left the cell, pushing the door shut behind her. It closed with a click and when Woland opened his eyes to look at her, she simply said, "I wouldn't give you the satisfaction of dying at my hands, Woland."

CHAPTER XIII
MYSTICAL OBSCENITIES

LILITH, NAKAM, AND Assistance Unlimited—Lazarus, Abigail, Morgan, Eun, The Black Terror, Samantha, and Kelly—were all gathered in a room that had, in the building's past history as a hotel, served as the ballroom. The large room's furniture had been hauled to the various walls, leaving a bare area in which Abby had drawn a massive pentagram. Candles were lit and placed along each point of the design.

Morgan stood near Samantha and Eun, all three of them armed to the teeth. Morgan held a tommy gun in both hands, while Samantha was armed with a revolver and had a knife strapped to her slim waist. Eun had daggers sheathed at both hips and all of them had selected weapons that had been blessed in holy water or featured silver-tipped bullets and points.

"You look tense," Samantha whispered to Morgan. Lazarus was consulting with Lilith and Abby about the specifics of whatever ritual was about to occur—all the majority of the team knew was that they were to prepare for a mission that involved the supernatural and which, if successful, would turn the tide in the current crisis.

"I am," he admitted. "It's bad enough that we've been fighting dead people all for the past 24 hours…but I can't help wondering if I'll see Mary again. Hopefully if I do, it'll be her spirit again and not as one of those…things."

Samantha nodded. She'd had similar thoughts of her own and she was sure that almost everyone else had, too. Her immediate family were all still alive but her grandpa had died a few years back and she couldn't stop wondering if his body was lumbering around somewhere out there, wreaking havoc. She hoped not but if all the dead were rising, surely he was.

Eun overheard this exchange but he didn't say anything. Aside from his mother and father, the rest of his family were in Korea. It hadn't really occurred to him how lucky he really was. He hadn't lost any of his closest friends or family—they had all survived the many bizarre occurrences of the past few years. He felt something akin to guilt when he thought about the losses suffered by some of the people in this room. It put his situation with his sexuality being outed to the public in perspective.

"If I could have everyone's attention," Lazarus said and all eyes turned towards him. He was a natural leader in that he had a way of commanding a room—he didn't need to raise his voice to cut through all other conversation and the way he simply assigned tasks without offering platitudes somehow spoke volumes about his belief that you could accomplish the impossible. "Woland's words have made me feel a bit foolish—because I should have foreseen the path we would need to walk. Four years ago, I escaped from the realm of the dead and in order to do so, I had to confront the woman known as Baba Yaga. I'm sure that most of you are at least somewhat familiar with the legends surrounding her—it's said that she lives where fear and wisdom meet, straddling the gap between life and death. She holds the secrets to both[10]. Like Woland, she sometimes goes by other names—Jezda or Jazi Baba, for instance. She's an unusual woman, even for a witch. Her teeth, nose and breasts are made of iron and her hair is formed of snakes. Furthermore, she moves through the forests using a gigantic mortar and pestle and she lives in a house that sits on chicken legs. The legs allow her house to rise up and move to safer locations during times of trouble.

"Is that all for real?" The Black Terror asked. "You're right—even for the sort of things we deal with, this crosses over into the absurd."

"It gets worse," Abby said. With a grin that she flashed at Lazarus, she added, "There's a fence around her house that's made out of the bones of people that made her angry! She's not all bad, though. She not

10 As told in volume six—specifically in the story entitled "The Strands of Fate."

only has dominion over death but also fertility, fate and nature. She can give great wisdom thanks to her power of prophecy…but it's difficult to find her and even harder to please her."

"You did it once before, right?" Morgan asked. "So she's already a fan of yours."

Lazarus shook his head. "I don't think it works like that. I had to fight my old enemy Walther Lunt for her amusement—the winner got to return to life, the loser went back to Hell. I'm only here because I won."

The Black Terror put a hand atop the handle of his sheathed cutlass. "So we're doing exactly what? We track her down and try to bargain with her to see if she'll reverse all this? Can she do that?"

"That's what we're going to find out," Lazarus responded. "The journey, as Abby said, won't be an easy one. Kelly and Nakam are going to stay here and man the fort while we're going. I've already spoken to the local authorities, as well as Daye, McCall, and Gravedigger. They know we're going to be out of town for a bit."

"And she's coming with us…why?" The Black Terror asked, nodding in the direction of Lilith.

The Mother of Monsters stepped forward, obviously not needing Lazarus to come to her defense. "It's never polite to bring up a woman's age but since I'm the one doing it, I guess it's all right to point out that I've been around for a long time… Lazarus here has met Baba Yaga once but I've dined with her in that chicken-legged house nearly a dozen times. Not only do we have what's probably the closest she gets to a friendship…we're also relatives. She's one of my many descendants."

"So hopefully she'll listen to you, even if she won't to Lazarus," Samantha said.

"We're trying to not take any chances," Lazarus confirmed. "That's why you're all going in armed, too. Now…any further questions before Abby sends us on our way?"

When no one spoke up, Lazarus turned and gave his wife a quick kiss before gesturing for everyone else to join him and Abby in the center of the pentagram.

Kelly stepped back and shielded her eyes as a bright bluish-white glow began to surround Abigail. No matter how many times she witnessed the attractive brunette do these sorts of things, they still took Kelly's breath away. She heard Abby whispering something under her breath and she watched as the young witch swept her hands through the air in a series of delicate movements.

The glow flared brighter…and when Kelly's vision was once more able to make out the details of the room, she saw that her husband and his companions were gone.

"Come back home in one piece, Lazarus," she whispered.

⸙

WOLAND SAT IN his cell, his absolute silence matched only by the painful fury brewing in his blackened heart. He told himself that he hadn't really expected anything different…logically, he knew that Lilith wasn't going to proclaim that she'd missed him and wanted him back. So why was he so stung by her continued rejection?

"Women… What is that Desiderius Erasmus said about them? 'Women…can't live with them, can't live without them.' Truer words have never been spoken."

Slowly, the Wandering Jew turned his head. He couldn't see the speaker from where he was but he knew it was another prisoner that had addressed him. "Your name, sir?" he asked.

"Professor Lionel Thorne," came the reply.

"Ah, yes…the man who slew a half dozen women in the early part of '41.'" Woland said. "They say you're not only an Olympic-level athlete but also a genius with a penchant for the supernatural…allegedly."

"Allegedly?"

"Yes—but if you were half of all that they say you are, you would have escaped this place by now. Instead you're reduced to carrying on conversations with strangers."

"I broke three of Gray's ribs when he brought me in," Thorne replied with more than a hint of anger. Woland smiled—it was so easy to identify men's weaknesses. Thorne was an egotist and thus easily played. "I nearly killed Eun Jiwon in hand-to-hand combat *and* I temporarily bound Abigail Cross to my will with a love potion!"

"Impressive," Woland said, in a voice that suggested it was anything but. "Is there some reason aside from boredom that you have chosen to address me?"

"Just wondering why you're still here... I couldn't help but overhear some of the conversations you've had with Lazarus and your ex. I'm certain you could figure out a way to get out of here."

"There is no point," Woland admitted. "The world is falling to pieces and I am denied the freedom of the grave...or the bed of the woman I desire."

"I had no idea you were such a joke. You're seriously going to waste away in here just because some woman rejected you? You do realize the world is filled with others that are just as beautiful if not more? Women are meant to be used and discarded."

"There are no others like her," Woland stood and grunted, his joints aching. "And who are you to insult me? You talk about how impressive you were in battle with Assistance Unlimited but here you are now... locked away. Just like me."

"I'm here by choice," Thorne claimed. "I'll be free again at some point...but I'm waiting for the right time."

"Of course." Woland paused and then asked, "Your love potion...it worked even on a woman as powerful as Abby Cross?"

"It did. She would have been mine forever if Lazarus hadn't forced me to tell him the counter-formula. I designed it myself...proof of my genius!"

"Tell me how to make it," Woland whispered. "Tell me...and I'll take you with me when I leave here."

Thorne paused. "I don't need your help."

"I'm certain you don't. Still, I would like your formula and I would want to repay you." Woland smiled softly, moving in for the kill. "A man of your intellect could be very valuable to me."

With a satisfied tone, Thorne responded, "It's good to find someone that appreciates my skills. I'll help you, Woland…but not as a servant. We shall be partners! Agreed?"

"My friend, I wouldn't have it any other way."

CHAPTER XIV
BABA YAGA!

THE SPELL DID not go as planned.

Abigail Cross had done similar things on numerous occasions—transporting herself and others across space and time—and never had anything gone wrong. In fact, she considered the spell a relatively simple one…

This time, she sensed that something was wrong almost immediately but it was too late to stop things from going forward. It was the equivalent of psychic turbulence that slammed into her, causing her to grunt in surprise. When the ritual ended and she found herself standing in the middle of a fog-enshrouded jungle, she looked about and felt her heart drop…standing near her was Eun, Morgan, and Samantha. There was no sign of Lazarus, Lilith, or The Black Terror.

"Where's everyone else?" Morgan asked, spinning about.

"I don't know," Abby replied.

"It felt like we were caught up in a gust of wind or something," Eun muttered. "I've never felt anything like that before when you've used that spell on us."

"I bet it was Lilith," Morgan said, reaching up to smooth out his moustache. It was a nervous habit of his. "I knew we shouldn't have brought her along."

"We don't know that," Samantha replied. "Lazarus said he trusted her."

"And so do I," Abby said. She took several deep breaths and added, "All we can do right now is figure out if we're in the right place—if we are, we go ahead and look for Baba Yaga. The others can take care of themselves."

"I don't recall anybody putting you in charge," Morgan said.

"You have a better idea?" Abby said, turning to face him.

"Yeah—use that magic of yours to look for Lazarus and the others. If Lilith has betrayed them, they might need our help!"

"Guys," Eun whispered.

"No, let me handle this," Morgan said. He stepped up to Abby and looked down his nose at her. "I've got seniority around here and I say we focus on our friends first."

Abby held up one finger in front of Morgan's face. "It would take time for me to locate them—if it's possible at all. That's time we'd be wasting when we could be saving Sovereign and the rest of the world from the walking dead, remember? We can look for Lazarus and the rest *after* we find out if Baba Yaga is around here."

"Guys!" Eun said, raising his voice a bit.

Samantha grabbed hold of Morgan's sleeve and gave it a tug. "Listen to Eun…"

Morgan and Abby both looked at Eun, who was staring up into the trees. They followed his gaze and froze in place—they were not alone here. Furry creatures were above them, watching them with wide eyes. They were about the size of monkeys but their tails ended in sharp barbs, their fur was a mix of blue and white, and when they opened their mouths to screech at the humans below, they revealed sharp teeth that glistened wetly.

"How about we table the discussion for now and focus on getting out of the forest?" Samantha asked.

No one bothered to reply verbally—they all took off running, following Eun's lead. The simian creatures began chattering and screaming, with some leaping from the trees to pursue the fleeing humans on the ground. Others remained above, leaping from limb to limb in an attempt to keep pace.

———⊶⊷⊷———

LAZARUS, LILITH AND Bob were just as confused—and in just as much danger.

The trio had materialized in the middle of an ancient, vine and moss-covered cemetery. The headstones were toppled over and the graves themselves were showing obvious signs of disturbance…the earth was churned up and in several spots splintered coffins had been shoved or dragged up from below.

The resurrected dead had been milling about when the heroes suddenly arrived in their midst but they turned as one and lunged towards them. The corpses were quite old, their clothes having mostly been reduced to aged rags. These things were mostly skeletons with just a few shrunken bits of skin or hair remaining.

The Black Terror responded without hesitation. When one of the dead grabbed hold of his cape, Bob thrust a closed fist right through the thing's head. It shattered in a cloud of dust and the rest of the body fell to the ground. The Black Terror crunched its ribs under his boots as he moved forward to grasp the arms of an undead female—he ripped them off her body and used them to pummel her to a dusty pile of bones.

Lilith was only a fraction of a second slower. She withdrew her Auray Rondel dagger and spun it through the air before burying it in the belly of a ghoul wearing the remnants of a black suit and top hat. She yanked it free and turned, lopping the head off another creature that was rushing towards her.

Lazarus Gray might have lacked the speed of his peers but he was just as effective. His pistol fired three bullets, felling three enemies in the process—each bullet lodged in the brains of the undead and their movements ceased immediately thereafter. "Headshots seem to work best," he shouted.

The din of battle, punctuated by the groans of his enemies, made it impossible to tell if Bob or Lilith heard him. Lazarus was confident that both would make the same discovery eventually so he chose to focus on what he could control: when he ran out of bullets, he holstered his gun and drew a hunting knife that he'd had sheathed at his waist. This forced him into closer fighting than he would have liked and the undead succeeded in tearing and scratching his flesh in a dozen places. Small rivulets of red began to flow across his body but it was lost amid the gore of the dead that flew about him as he hacked away at them.

"Stop!"

The female voice, cracked with age, resounded through the graveyard with tremendous force. The shambling undead froze in place, heads creakily turning to face the direction of the woman that had spoken. Lilith didn't hesitate to take advantage of the situation, dispatching two more of her foes as soon as they stopped resisting.

A curious woman stood nearby, her skin hanging loosely on her arms but exceedingly taut on her face. Her scent—musky and slightly unpleasant—carried on the wind. She was dressed in a dark green shift that was more rag than clothing and she leaned heavily upon a gnarled walking stick whose tip was adorned with the skull of some small woodland creature. She ignored the dead as she crept closer, actually shoving one out of the way with the point of her stick. Her attention was fixed entirely upon Lazarus Gray. "*You*," she said, the word drawn out with obvious disdain.

"You remember me," Lazarus said. He sheathed his blade, glancing quickly at the walking dead, many of whom were now shambling away, having lost all interest in them. "Thank you for stopping the battle."

Baba Yaga waved a hand dismissively. "You destroy them like they're monsters…they are merely the insane dead. You would be no better in their position." She pointed a crooked finger at Lazarus. "Few men are foolish enough to seek me out twice. I told you last time that I was done with you."

"I'm not here by choice. The Wandering Jew has taken advantage of the weakening of the barriers between the living and the dead…and, yes, I know I've played a part in that, as well. He engineered a terrible tragedy and that brought the walls down—now the dead walk among the living and it's a plague that's spreading. I am hoping that you can help end this."

The old witch sneered and said, "And you know damned well that I don't do anything for free!" She shrugged her bony shoulders and added, "In this case, however, there is little I can do. The Quietus is too powerful for me to enslave. You'll have to do that yourself."

Lazarus looked at Lilith who gave a shake of her head. He didn't bother checking to see if Bob was familiar with this "Quietus" as he knew that The Black Terror had little knowledge of the supernatural and even less interest in it. "I don't know what that means," Lazarus admitted.

"Of course you don't," Baba said with a chuckle. She tugged at a few wisps of hair that dangled from her chin and then snapped her fingers. The ground began to shake as something massive pushed through the trees, knocking one or two over as it moved past.

The witch's house was suddenly before them, supported by mammoth chicken legs that then crouched into a sitting position, putting the front entrance slightly higher than the ground. As Lazarus watched, Baba bent her knees and sprang into the open doorway and turned back to face him. She blocked the opening in such a way that made it clear that he and his friends were to remain outside.

"The Quietus is an entity much like me—only far less attractive." Baba cackled at this, revealing a misshapen set of teeth that were in dire need of dental care. "I have dominion over life and death, as you know… but there are creatures that exist in-between these states. Those belong to The Quietus. Their numbers were always few so his power was kept in check—that is no longer the case. Now I grow weaker as the living become the dead…but are then resurrected to serve The Quietus. If you plan to return these abominations to their proper state of being, there is only one path available to you: you must find and destroy The Quietus. It will be a temporary victory in one way—he will reform within hours, but in that time all the resurrected will have their souls cast back beyond the veil of the living and I will be able to restore the breaches that have been caused."

The Black Terror nodded, visibly pleased—if all that was needed involved punching something, he was more than ready. "How do we find this thing?"

Baba Yaga pointed towards the west, where the sun was setting. "You won't have any trouble finding him. He is huge now and he is feeling confident. He will not hide in the shadows any longer. He thinks it is his time—and perhaps it is."

Lilith wiped the blood off her blade, using a strip of cloth from one of the fallen corpses. "I expect to live to see the End Times, old woman—but I don't think these are them. We'll find your Quietus... and we'll gut it like a fish. You and I have a history and you know that I speak the truth always."

"Your confidence speaks well of you," Baba Yaga replied. "You have ever been a strong woman and a true ally."

"Then give us something to help us win," Lilith replied. "Don't just squat there like a frog on her lily pad—give us a weapon or a boon! Tell us how to destroy The Quietus and give you your power back."

The witch grunted but said nothing for a moment. When she finally spoke, she said, "Your strongman's blade has been replaced with one that I have enchanted. That alone will be enough to pierce the heart of The Quietus. Now go! I have no more words to aid you!"

The house turned about, moving away on its strange chicken legs. When it had walked out of sight, Lazarus turned to Bob and gestured for him to draw his cutlass.

The Black Terror pulled his sword from its scabbard and the blade gleamed with a piercing green-tinted light that illuminated the growing darkness. This was a light capable of driving away devils...and Bob could feel a strange power spreading from the hand that gripped the sword's hilt. The power moved along his arm and finally took root in his inhuman heart, pulsing and growing.

"How do you feel?" Lilith asked.

"Like I could slay a giant," The Black Terror replied. "Or the devil himself."

CHAPTER XV
HOME IS WHERE THE KILLERS ARE

KELLY STEPPED INTO the monitor room carrying a cup of steaming coffee in her hands. She had just put the kids to bed—both Emily and Ezekiel had been especially rambunctious tonight and as a result they were going to sleep hard.

She sat down in front of the oversized television screens that showed live images of Robeson Avenue. One of the screens had a small dot in the corner that was flashing, indicating that something had recently set off its motion sensor.

Setting aside her coffee, she leaned forward and studied the image. A tall man wearing an overcoat was walking straight towards the front door of her home. Pursing her lips, she reached out and touched a few controls. The image shifted, drawing in closer to the stranger—he had a well-chiseled face, with prominent cheekbones and a slightly cruel turn to his lips. He looked somewhat flushed, like he'd been exerting himself profusely and there was something unnatural about his gait, like he was straining somehow.

"Captain Krieger."

Kelly's head whipped around and she saw that Alf was standing in the doorway. He had stopped wearing that white mask of his, which she appreciated—she found it very disturbing when he wore it. "This is the Nazi that asked you to find Karl?"

"It is." Alf moved forward, coming to stand next to Kelly's chair. Onscreen, Krieger had reached the front door. He read the sign that directed visitors to push the buzzer and he followed the directions, resulting in a high-pitched sound filling the office.

Ignoring it for the moment, Kelly asked, "How did he trace you here?"

"I don't know—maybe he called in a favor from someone at the OFP." The buzzer sounded once more and Alf turned to leave the room. "I'll put my face back on and meet him at the door. Tell him to wait a second...and warn Karl and his cousin."

Kelly nodded, flipping the switch that allowed her to speak to Krieger. "Someone will be with you shortly. Please remain where you are."

In heavily accented English, the Nazi officer replied, "Believe me, Fräulein, that I have no intention of leaving this site."

With a frown, Kelly sat back in her chair. She didn't like this—why would Krieger walk so boldly up to the door of the Assistance Unlimited's headquarters? He must have something up his sleeve, she reasoned.

Realizing that she hadn't yet warned The Puzzler, she did so...and kept her eyes glued to the screen that showed Nakam opening the front door.

KRIEGER'S EYES WIDENED somewhat as the spectral figure of Nakam stepped into view. The legendary "Jewish Avenger" had been dismissed by some in the Nazi hierarchy but Krieger had never doubted the man's existence—but to see him here, in America...that was a surprise. "Nakam," the German said in his native language. "Have you fled to America at last?"

Ignoring the question, Nakam replied with one of his own. "Why are you here, Herr Krieger? If you're seeking Karl Harmatz, he's no longer a concern of yours. He's been reunited with his cousin."

"And what of Alf Lindemann? If you know about Karl, then you must know about Alf…I sent him to find Herr Harmatz and he's gone missing. Is he here too? Or did you kill him, as you have so many other good Nazis?"

Nakam paused, wondering just how much Krieger knew. Had his identity been revealed at last? Knowing Krieger, he doubted it—the Captain had never been good at holding back from gloating and if he'd figured out that Alf was the notorious Nakam, he would have said so by now. Choosing to bluff his way out of the situation, Nakam replied, "He's here. Given his position, I thought he might have some useful information to share with us…but he's been remarkably tight-lipped."

Krieger pursed his lips and nodded. "I've always liked him, that Lindemann. In fact, I've always thought he was wasted in that office. He's a killer, I can tell. Like recognizes like."

Grateful that the mask hid his expression, Alf asked, "So are you going to leave now, Captain? There's nothing more for you to do. The Silver Coins—yes, I know all about them—have been locked away. Neither you nor the Fuehrer can get to them."

"I consulted with Karl Ernst Krafft before coming here—do you know him?"

Somewhat taken aback by the change in subject, Nakam merely answered with a shake of his head. He heard a squelching sound as Krieger shifted his weight from foot to foot—the man's boots were wet, though it wasn't raining.

"He successfully predicted the bomb that went off at a Munich beer hall in 1939—it was only through divine providence that Hitler left the scene scant moments before. Krafft was brought onboard to serve as the Reich's official astrologer…until Rudolph Hess made his absurd flight to Scotland. Since Hess was such a big supporter of Krafft and others like him, the Fuehrer decided in his fury to have many occultists rounded up and thrown into prison. That's where I found him—he's going quite mad, I think. He's developed a terrible persecution complex. He did a reading for me and it told me to come here to find the coins and our missing friends. He didn't mention you, though. I suppose no one is perfect, eh?" Krieger drew in a shuddering breath and Nakam noticed the way the German's face constricted in an expression of pain.

Realizing that the Jewish vigilante had seen this, Krieger continued, "I met with some resistance on the way over here—there's a large number of undead wandering the city streets."

"How badly hurt are you?" Nakam asked, surprised at himself for feeling concern. Krieger was the sort of Nazi that he usually killed... but he supposed that he didn't generally have any kind of personal connection to his foes and this time he did. "If you die inside the city, you could come back as one of those things," he added.

Krieger pulled open his overcoat, revealing that his clothing was soaked with blood. His midsection was ripped and torn, revealing his intestines, which were tied in place by what looked like wire. "I did take a pretty bad flesh wound, I have to admit. Did a small amount of in-the-field surgery to stitch myself back together." He smiled and Nakam saw death and madness in that grin. What in the world was keeping this man on his feet? Had he already begun to change...? Was he even now crossing over from living to dead?"

"That's a bit more than a flesh wound, Herr Krieger." Nakam drew his blade. "I can put you out of your misery...and I swear that I won't let you come back as a monster."

"How kind of you." Krieger took one wet-sounding step closer to Nakam and leaned in slightly, as if sharing a secret. "If you really want to help, you can give me the coins. If they're as powerful as I've heard, maybe they can do something about this." He gestured with one bloody hand towards his torso. A little bit of blood dripped to the ground, vanishing beneath Krieger's boot—and Nakam suddenly realized why the man had made so much noise when he walked.

"They don't work that way," Nakam said. "Nothing good comes from them."

"I don't think I'll take your word for that," Krieger replied. He threw himself at Nakam, slamming the slightly smaller man against the door to the building. Up close the smell of death was almost palpable and Alf fought the urge to retch as he felt something warm and wet slam against his midsection...he knew it was Krieger's tightly bound entrails. "You smell good enough to eat," the Nazi hissed into Nakam's ear. He snapped his teeth together, as if warming to the idea of tearing into his opponent's flesh.

Nakam drove his knife into the Captain's belly, slicing into his exposed guts. He twisted the blade and then slashed it left to right. The actions were enough to weaken the wire binding them together and they spilled out, slapping against Nakam's body before landing with a wet smack on the ground.

Krieger hissed and his eyes became glassy—and Nakam realized that he was right: the Nazi had already been on the cusp of death and how he'd fully passed over…which meant that the threat was hardly over.

The German wrapped his hands about Nakam's throat and pulled the vigilante closer. Krieger's mouth was open, allowing foul breath to spill out, and his teeth were closing in for a bite. Even as Nakam struggled to get free, he continued to plunge his knife in and out of the Nazi but it seemed to have little effect.

Alf felt his body beginning to shut down—Krieger's supernatural-born strength was cutting off his oxygen and no matter how hard he slashed with his blade, the Nazi grew ever closer to ripping his throat out. He silently prayed that he would be reunited with his loved ones on the other side eventually…but he knew that if he died now, he would first have to suffer the madness and bloodlust of the undead plague.

Just when things looked their bleakest, Krieger's head exploded in a crack of loud noise, drenching Nakam's face-mask in gore. He shook his head, backing away, which allowed Krieger's corpse to topple over. Turning to his right, he saw a beautiful Negro woman clad in a red bodysuit. She held a smoking revolver and had a smug expression on her face. "You looked like you needed a bit of help," she said in English.

Wiping a gloved hand over his mask to clear away the blood from the eye holes, Nakam gave a brief nod. "I won't pretend that I didn't. You're one of the Crimson Ladies?"

"Captain Arjana. It's my airship that's on the rooftop." She lowered her voice somewhat and added, "You're the one that killed my sisters in Berlin."

"To be fair, they tried to kill me first." Nakam rubbed at his neck, which ached terribly. He could only imagine the bruises that were forming. "How did you know I was in trouble?"

"I told my crew that I needed to stretch my legs. I was having a cigarette around the back of the building when I heard you talking to this one… You shouldn't have killed him. It only made him more dangerous." Arjana reached into the fold of her jumpsuit and pulled out a small container of smokes. She offered it to Nakam who shook his head.

"Thanks but no… My throat already feels like it's on fire."

"And you are called Nakam?" she asked.

"That's right. For what it's worth, I'm sorry for the misunderstanding in Berlin. I suppose I should have teamed up with your friends but it seemed to me that they posed a threat to Karl and I was trying to keep him safe."

The Nubian moved closer, smiling a bit. "It's actually alright…all of us know that we could die at any moment and we have accepted that. At least they died in battle. I'm rather impressed that a single man could have dealt with them, to be honest. Would you like to come up to the airship after we dump this corpse and tell me the details? I'd love to hear how you did it."

Alf froze—was she flirting with him? He was positive she was, though it had been long enough in between romances that he almost doubted himself. Here he was, covered in gore…and she was inviting him up to her place? To swap stories about killing her friends?

She *was* lovely, though.

And he *was* lonely, if truth be told.

Before he even realized it, he was saying, "Lead the way."

THE PUZZLER HAD reacted to Kelly's warning with appropriate haste. He'd slipped from the sheets that he'd been sharing with his cousin, pulled on his costume, and then plucked up a wooden chair which he smashed against the wall until one of its legs came off in jagged fashion.

Karl sat up, pulling the sheets tight against his naked body, and stared. "You look ridiculous in that outfit," he whispered. "But scary, too."

With a crooked grin, The Puzzler responded, "Thanks, love…I won't let Krieger hurt you. You have my word on that. I just can't believe he came all this way. He's probably more interested in the coins than he is in you or I, though."

Kelly's voice emerged from the intercom once more, saying, "Stand down, boys. It looks like Nakam has handled it…with a little bit of help, anyways."

"Well, damn," The Puzzler said, letting his shoulders slump. "I was kind of looking forward to smashing his head in."

"My hero," Karl said with a chuckle. He noticed that his cousin was remaining in his costume, looking pensive. "Are you okay?"

"Just wondering if I should make a play for those coins myself." He looked over at Karl and added, "They're powerful…and a lot of people would pay just to have a single one of them. We'd be on easy street, Karl. We could live like kings!"

"I don't want to live like a king…I just want to live." Karl pushed away the sheets, revealing a thin, almost emaciated body. "Look at me. They were going to kill me eventually—and they'd kill every Jew in the entire world if they could. I just want to find a nice house near a stream, with nice weather…and I want you to be there with me."

Ronald took a deep breath and sat on the edge of the bed. "I've done some awful things, Karl. I'm not the man you remember. If you knew the real me, I don't think you'd be asking me to run off with you."

"I'm no saint, either, Ronald." Karl stood up and embraced his cousin, who returned the hug with equal fervor. "But if we're going to stay together, you can't keep playing the villain... I'm done looking over my shoulder, expecting the authorities to come calling and drag me away—and I won't be fretting over you, either. Can you agree to that?"

"There's a good chance that The Black Terror will throw me in prison for some things I did just before you got here...but after that, I can promise that I'll try. Is that good enough?"

Karl shook his head but he was smiling at the same time. "No... trying isn't good enough. You have to actually do it. I'll help you, though."

CHAPTER XVI
THE REVENANT

THE QUARTET CONSISTING of Abby Cross, Morgan Watts, Eun Jiwon, and Samantha Grace were beginning to slow but their pursuers showed no signs of giving up the chase. In fact, Eun was positive that the simian monsters were herding them somewhere, forcing them towards some unknown point—and he trembled at the thought of where that might be.

They had been moving towards the deeper recesses of the jungle and the sun was increasingly blotted out by the thick canopy over their heads. It was Morgan that first tripped, his foot catching over a thick root that he hadn't seen in the gloom. He fell forward and it took a moment for his companions to realize that their friend wasn't with them.

Samantha spun about, being the first to notice that Morgan wasn't beside her. She saw him struggling to his feet, wincing as he put pressure on his left ankle. The monkeys were very close to him, several of them within an arm's reach—a half dozen had slowed to a stop when he fell and were quickly forming a circle about him while their brethren continued to chase the others.

"Morgan!" she shouted. One of the creatures that had been chasing her now leapt through the air and struck her hard in the chest. It began beating at her with its little fists, screeching all the while. She grabbed hold of it and shoved it away, pleased to hear it cry out in pain as it hit the ground.

Eun and Abby realized what had happened and turned to help. They saw Morgan vanish underneath a mob of the little beasts and heard him cursing as his skin was struck by fists, claws, and teeth. Abby launched several small bursts of lightning at the nearest of the creatures, allowing Eun and Samantha to make it closer to Morgan.

With a spinning kick, Eun broke the neck of one blue-furred monkey that had been snapping at Morgan's legs. Samantha dispatched another by firing her small handgun at point-blank range. The little fellow's brains exploded out a pea-sized hole in its head and fell over.

Morgan was doing his best to free himself of the horde, as well. He grabbed hold of the creatures by whatever he could seize, be it throat, tail or arm, and hurled them with all his might.

The eldest member of Assistance Unlimited would have been horrified to view himself in a mirror—his normally spotless attire was covered in dirt and was torn in a dozen places. His hair stuck up at all angles and there were small scratches on his face and neck, revealing tiny streaks of blood.

Samantha caught her friend as he swayed on his feet, still unable to put his full weight on his ankle. "Lean on me, Morgan," she whispered.

"Just leave me—I'm slowing you down."

"Don't be stupid," she spat out, blinking as Eun punched a monkey right out of the air as it jumped towards her face.

"They're leaving," Abby said, hurrying to join her friends. For the first time, Eun noticed that the simians were slinking back into the trees...but why? They had the humans in an enclosed area, with one of them injured...why back off now?

"We were led here," Eun said, looking around. "And now that we're here, they don't have to chase us anymore."

"What are you talking about?" Samantha asked, struggling to help hold up Morgan. She was tempted to ask Eun to take over but she didn't want to appear weak—and, besides, she thought Eun should offer without being asked anyway.

"They are smarter than they appear," a man's voice said, seeming to come from all around them. "They led you here because they know you to be outsiders…and all newcomers to Bordia must gain my permission to be allowed to stay."

"Bordia? Where the hell is that?" Morgan wondered aloud.

Eun answered with a shrug but it was Abby that asked, "And who are you? Are you the king or chief of this place?"

A figure dropped down from above, landing in a crouch before slowly rising to his feet. He wore a fearsome black bodysuit that included a skull cap, a domino mask, and twin-holstered handguns. "I am more than any mere king or chief," the stranger declared. "I am The Revenant."

DEEP WITHIN THE tiny African nation of Bordia lay a cave of wondrous design. Mother Nature had, through centuries of rain and wind, shaped the cave's entrance so that it resembled nothing less than a humanoid skull, its mouth forming the entrance to the lair within. The local tribes dubbed this cave "The Revenant's Lair," for it was said to be the abode of a man who had lived continuously since the late 1400s when a European sailor had been thrown overboard during a treacherous mutiny. The man had been found by friendly natives, who aided him in hiding his survival behind a mask. He had become The Revenant, striking back at his betrayers by becoming one with the jungle he now called home. He stalked them like a hunter would his prey and eventually brought them to a violent sort of justice.

In the years since, The Revenant had adopted the cave as his private residence. Though the natives attributed his constant appearances over the years to immortality, the truth was that he had married a woman while visiting family in England, bringing her back to Bordia. Their son had eventually become the second Revenant and through the years more descendants had done the same, all operating with the same weapons and attire—a fearsome black bodysuit, skullcap and domino mask.

The current Revenant was the 22nd in the line. Born with the name Lee Pence, he was as young and fit as his father and his father before him. But his greatest attribute was the keen mind he possessed, which allowed him to outthink enemies of all types.

In the section of the cave dwelling that he used as his library, The Revenant now sat before a mixture of herbs that were slowly burning, their smoke enveloping his masked face. His guests from Assistance Unlimited sat on chairs formed by wooden sticks bound together by fronds.

Elsewhere in the home his wife and two children—both girls— were cleaning up after dinner. Because there had never been a female Revenant, he and his wife had tried repeatedly for a son. A woman dressed in The Revenant costume would doubtlessly destroy the legend of an immortal jungle protector[11]...it would become clear that the most recent Revenant had not in fact been the original but rather just the latest in a long line of human warriors.

And the legend had power, no doubt of that. Thus, a son was needed before it was too late. Already, The Revenant could feel middle age looming over him...he would grow slow and inevitably die. There had to be someone to follow in his footsteps...

The Revenant sighed, pushing such dark thoughts away.

He looked around his home and smiled. Despite the fact that he lived in the jungle, The Revenant kept a well-furnished abode that looked every bit as comfortable as any suburban house in America. His children sometimes accompanied him on journeys to the so-called "civilized countries" but what they had seen only confirmed that their father was right to spurn the Western nations in favor of his jungle home: the trappings of civilization only seemed to inspire men to even greater crimes, which they could then cover up with meaningless words like "progress."

"How are you feeling, my friend?" The Revenant asked, directing the question at Morgan. He spoke English flawlessly and Samantha had already asked him how many languages he spoke fluently and learned that he could converse in six different tongues, along with a number of minor jungle dialects.

---

11 As "Death From the Jungle," a story featuring The Peregrine set in 1943, showed, this is far from the truth. One of Lee's daughters becomes the first female Revenant and she eventually became a member of The Claws of The Peregrine.

Lifting up his left ankle, which was tightly wrapped with a poultice, Morgan offered a grin. "It feels so much better. I don't know what's in this thing but the pain went away almost immediately."

"It's a mixture of various plants and gazelle dung," the jungle hero replied, one corner of his mouth twitching upward as he saw the expression of shock on Morgan's face. "It's very effective for deadening pain and helping heal small wounds."

"Dung… You mean you put animal shit on my leg?" Morgan asked. He glanced quickly at Abby and Samantha, adding, "Sorry, ladies."

Samantha's snort prompted the rest of the group—including The Revenant—to burst out in laughter.

When everyone had calmed down, Abby turned her attention to their masked host. He had earlier shared some of his past with them while Morgan's leg was being tended by one of The Revenant's servants but he hadn't given away all his secrets, leaving Abby with a few questions. "I don't sense any magical energy surrounding you or this lair," she said, "but something drew us off-course. We were supposed to end up in Europe with our friends. Do you have any idea what might have led us to end up here?"

After a moment's consideration, The Revenant rose from his seat and nodded. He stood with his hands on his hips, looking every bit the heroic figure. "I think I just might. If Morgan feels up to it, how about we take a small hike up the side of the mountain? There's something up there that I think all of you should see."

"I can keep up—just don't blame me if I start smelling like I've stepped in something foul," Morgan said with a grin. "Because that's sort of the case."

Eun gave a playful shove on Morgan's shoulder. "Don't worry about it, old man. You don't smell any different than usual."

"Thanks, kid. You really know how to make a guy feel good about himself."

Samantha smiled at her friends' interplay but she caught a glimpse of a young girl peeking around the corner, watching the scene with interest. When she realized she'd been spotted, the girl vanished from sight. Samantha glanced up to see The Revenant watching her.

"That's one of my daughters—Sally," the masked man said. "She's a big fan of those pulp magazines that recount stories of Assistance Unlimited, The Peregrine, and Gravedigger. I'm sure she recognizes the lot of you."

"Maybe I can say hello to her when we return," Samantha offered.

Nodding, The Revenant thanked her and then said to the rest of the group, "Shall we?" He gestured towards the door and led the way out into the night air.

⎯⎯⎯∞∞∞⎯⎯⎯

A SOFT RAIN had begun to fall as the group moved up the side of the mountain. The earth slipped under their feet and Samantha found herself helping Abby at one point when the brunette nearly lost her balance. The two women held on to each other for support and Samantha took the opportunity to whisper, "Don't take it personal with Morgan—you know how he gets sometimes."

Abby looked at her in confusion and then her eyes widened. "Oh! I'd completely forgotten about that argument we had when we first got here. I know that he's just grumpy when he's worried." She gave a shrug of her shoulders. "Besides, he and I butt heads all the time... I don't think he really likes strong-willed women."

"He and I have always gotten along just fine," Samantha pointed out. Abby didn't say anything for a moment, prompting Samantha to ask, "Unless you're trying to say that I'm not strong-willed like you are...?"

"We just have different styles, that's all," Abby said. "You're tough as nails but you can also bat your eyelashes and play the demure girl when it's necessary. Morgan likes that and you know exactly when to do it... I've never had that knack. I'm a lot more direct and I never really turn that off."

"I'm not sure if you're giving me a compliment or just really good at side-stepping an insult," Samantha replied with a chuckle.

"I envy you," Abby admitted. "You're glamorous but men respect you. I've always felt that they don't take me seriously unless I work three times as hard."

"Honey, we all feel that way—because it's true." Samantha gave her friend a little hug but their conversation ended when they realized that The Revenant had stopped walking. They had reached their destination, it seemed—the mist suddenly ended, leaving them all damp and a little bit chilled.

The group stood facing a strangely-shaped tree, one whose bark was almost as dark as the night sky. The thick trunk rose up straight from the ground before suddenly twisting around and around, limbs branching off from it. The leaves were irregular in appearance, almost as if many of them should have been on another tree entirely. A musky scent filled the air and tiny bits of white fluff seemed to float from the limbs, swirling around the members of Assistance Unlimited, as if borne on some wind that none of them could feel. At the base of the tree was a gnarled set of roots that had burst up from the earth, forming a weblike mass that had openings large enough for a small man or a petite woman to slip through…though given the unearthly aura surrounding the strange tree, none of those assembled gave any thought to trying to do so.

Morgan said the words that all of them were thinking—"That's the damndest tree I've ever seen."

The Revenant knelt at the foot of the tree, staring down into the portal that lay between the roots. "One of my ancestors claim that this tree took root after an evil man died here. It sprouted up the very next day, as if his blood had watered some seed that had lain unseen for centuries. He called it the Grendel Tree and he said that there were others like it, in secret corners of the world and that stories were told that it would let loose these bits of fluff when it was ready to take someone on a journey." He glanced up at Abby, stretching out a palm that was soon covered by the tiny white objects, which on close inspection looked like flecks of snow and said, "It started producing these things early this morning, just as the sun was coming into view. I wondered why but now

I think I know—it somehow led your group here because one of you is meant to crawl inside this hole."

"Excuse me?" Morgan scoffed. "Why in the name of heaven and earth would anybody do that?"

"Because it's magic," Abby replied. "I can sense it now that I'm close to it. It's old magic and I think it can't be denied."

"Oh yeah? What's it going to do if we all turn around and go back down the mountain?" Morgan asked.

"I imagine that all of you would meet grisly ends," The Revenant replied matter-of-factly.

Eun frowned and crossed his arms, asking, "What did you mean about this tree taking someone on a journey? So it's not just as simple as crawling around between a bunch of muddy roots?"

"No…people that have gone inside when the Petals of the Moon are flying say that they see powerful visions of those on the other side. Typically it's someone that has recently seen a loved one that has passed on that is summoned to the Grendel Tree.

Abby and Samantha both looked at Morgan, knowing of his encounter with the spirit of his sister.

"Assuming this is all on the up-and-up," Morgan said, after taking a deep breath, "then the tree wants me. Before all the craziness with the dead rising, I saw my sister Mary." He looked at The Revenant and added, "If I go digging around under there…will I see her again?"

"Wait a minute," Eun said. "He called this thing the Grendel Tree. Grendel was a monster that Beowulf fought, remember? And this thing grew from the blood of an evil man… What makes you think this is anything positive?"

"It won't harm you," The Revenant replied. "At least not physically. People who go through this emerge in a slightly changed state. They learn things that alter them…some people react poorly to this and they struggle with it. Others are empowered by the knowledge they obtain. I can't promise that you'll come out of this stronger than when you go in…but there's nothing inherently evil in the process. I think that the spirit of the man that died here does live on but he's in the process of redemption. This is the universe's way of making him atone for the awful things he did in life."

Morgan nodded, removing his wet coat and tossing it on the ground. He'd already reconciled himself to the fact that this suit was ruined beyond even Mr. Cho's ability to clean down at the local laundromat. "You didn't answer me before—will I see Mary again?"

"I don't know," the masked man admitted. "What you see is for you alone."

"Morgan," Samantha said, putting a hand on his arm. She was shocked to feel that he was trembling. "You don't have to do this, you know… None of us are afraid of any old death spell. We've faced worse."

"Don't you see, Sam? She might have brought me here—maybe it's the only way she can see me again. If she has something more to tell me, I need to hear it." Morgan forced a smile and leaned forward, planting a kiss on her forehead. "I'll be back in two shakes. Don't worry."

Morgan glanced at Eun—who was frowning in obvious disbelief that his friend was actually going along with this—and at Abby, who gave him a brief smile and a nod of her head. Stepping away from Samantha, he approached the Grendel Tree and asked, "So… I just start crawling in? I don't need to utter any magic words or anything?"

The Revenant shook his head and backed away, giving Morgan all the room that he needed. "Good luck," he said. "We'll wait for you."

Kneeling in the muck, Morgan wrinkled his nose and said, "I'm probably going to need a hot bath after this."

⸺◦✸◦⸺

THE PASSAGE WAS a tight fit for Morgan whose midsection had started to spread in recent years. He still cut a relatively trim figure but age had a way of broadening almost everyone and Morgan was no exception. He grunted as he forced his hips past a close-set grouping of roots. The soft earth beneath him suddenly gave way and he found himself sliding quickly forward, down into a pit of sorts under the tree. He landed in a heap, rolling over onto his back. Breathing rapidly, he stared up at the underside of the tree. The hollow was big enough that he could actually stand at his full height and he took advantage of this, rising to his feet with cracking joints.

He resisted the urge to brush off his clothing, knowing that it would only upset him—besides, this was the kind of dirty that nothing short of a bonfire would cure.

Squinting, Morgan examined his surroundings. It was surprisingly bright under here —and he couldn't tell where the light source came from it. It was as if the entire area were lit from all directions at once. The scene was quiet but not entirely—though he thought it his imagination, Morgan thought he could hear things crawling through the earthen walls all around him…insects, small creatures, things that called the dark, moist underground their home. He was an outsider here, a visitor to a strange land.

Taking a deep breath and feeling more than a little bit silly, Morgan asked, "Mary…? Are you here?"

"I'm here, Morgan…but you shouldn't turn around."

Morgan froze, relief and fear warring in his heart. It was her voice, all right, and it was coming from right behind him. The hair stood up on the nape of his neck and he felt a chill run through him, as if someone had opened the door to a walk-in freezer. "Why can't I see you?" he asked.

"I don't look the same as when you saw me last. It was hard enough to manifest then and it's even harder now. I was revived just like all the others, Morgan."

Clenching his hands into fists, Morgan asked, "Then how are you here now—?"

"A police officer shot me twice in the head…injuries to our heads causes our reanimated bodies to stop moving and sends our souls back to the afterlife. The problem is that the barriers are down now so those souls that are dispatched again are just floating loose…it's hard to remain sane and hard to manifest any kind of appearance at all. I'm afraid that if you saw me, it would taint your memories of me and I don't want that. So, please, don't turn around."

"I won't," Morgan promised. He would have agreed to almost anything she could have asked of him. He felt his eyes growing moist—it was so good to be near her again. "I've missed you so damned much," he admitted.

"I know… I've kept an eye on you. You worried me when you went down the wrong path but I always knew that you'd end up turning things around. I'm proud of you for what you've done with Assistance Unlimited."

"Thank you…" he whispered. He started to turn around but stopped himself. "Why did you want me to come here? Did you have something else to tell me?"

"Yes…and I'm sorry that I have to tell you this, Morgan, but I think you need to know." Morgan could sense that she was moving closer to him and he shivered as the cold in the air became more intense. He suddenly wished he hadn't tossed away his coat before climbing down here. Her icy breath filled his ear as she whispered so quietly that he was uncertain if he heard her correctly—he'd expected to hear something about his family or perhaps some dark secret from Mary's own life. Instead, she offered him information…about Lazarus?

Forgetting his earlier promise, he turned quickly, intending to ask her to repeat what she'd said…but he saw nothing save for the earthen walls that surrounded him. Mary was gone.

"Mary, please don't leave me—not so soon," he said. Taking a deep breath, he tried to focus on what she had told him, even though it made no sense whatsoever. Even if it were true, why had she thought it so important that he be told?

There is a secret room located behind the bookshelf in Lazarus Gray's study, she had said to him. *You need to see it—but whatever you do, don't tell anyone else about it.*

Sighing, Morgan the palms of his hands against his eyes in an attempt to squash the tears that threatened to flow. He tried to tell himself that he should just be glad that he'd been able to see her at all and that he was lucky to have not had to encounter her as one of those monsters that were running loose in Sovereign.

Don't tell anyone else about it.

Morgan would do as she asked, though he couldn't fathom why she'd asked him to do it. If Lazarus wanted to keep something to himself, he'd more than earned that right and Morgan would never begrudge him for it. He trusted Lazarus with his life...

So why did he feel like Mary's words were going to upset everything?

He began to crawl back out of the hole, thinking that he'd only spent about ten minutes under the Grendel Tree. He would soon find out that he'd been gone for more than two hours...but even when he heard that, he wouldn't share the details of what he'd seen or been told.

CHAPTER XVII
THE QUIETUS

LILITH AND LAZARUS led the way into the small village, their footsteps sounding loud on the cobblestone path. The Black Terror followed along behind, his newly empowered cutlass held in his right hand. He hadn't sheathed the blade since learning of its new power and Lazarus had noticed that the team's chemist kept staring at the blade, as if entranced by it.

Since leaving Baba Yaga, the trio had followed a trail of destruction that they'd discovered not far from where her house had vanished from view. Trees were overturned, animals slaughtered and a foul stench had led them to this town, nestled in a grass-covered valley. The area practically begged to be described as "quaint," but upon closer inspection that word transformed in the minds of the heroes to "horrible." Dead bodies were strewn about on the streets, doors into homes were broken and shattered, and a church steeple had been ripped off and embedded in the middle of the town square. A steaming pile of silver-colored excrement lay next to the steeple, offering what Lazarus assumed was The Quietus' view on religion.

A loud roar, unlike any that Lazarus had ever heard before, echoed through the village. It seemed to start somewhere to the north but it was difficult to pin down given the way that it bounced off the buildings.

Lilith placed a hand on Lazarus' shoulder. "I can't help but wonder why she gave the super-weapon to your lieutenant and not to you."

Lazarus gave an unconcerned shrug. "I don't care who kills The Quietus as long as it's done—he's the strongest of us so perhaps she thought that would play a part."

"When all this is over, I would like to have the chance to talk to you in private."

Lazarus glanced at her, his eyes flicking down to her hand and then back to her face. Though his expression didn't change, something made her draw her hand away. "I know that you're attracted to me," he said matter-of-factly, "and I would be a liar if I didn't acknowledge your own appeal, both physically and intellectually…but I am quite happily married."

For a moment, Lilith looked stung but then she smiled and her eyes shone prettily. "Not many men reject me—but I think you might have misunderstood. I *am* attracted to you but I wouldn't try to break up another woman's marriage. My feelings of sisterhood are too strong for that…but you and I are more alike than most people I meet. I thought we could swap stories and maybe form some sort of alliance. Believe it or not, my Crimson Ladies are heroes, too. We try to protect the world from things that would eat people alive, figuratively and literally."

"I've heard that your Ladies sometimes kill lots of people—innocent people that just happen to be caught in the crossfire. My team tries to avoid that. If we were going to work together, you'd have to curb your methods."

With a short laugh, Lilith said, "You do realize that I'm practically immortal, right? My 'methods' as you call them are a product of all the centuries I've been alive. You're viewing me through a set of morals that are based in one specific point in time—your lifetime. Laws and ethics change and evolve…and I try to keep up with those changes…but when it comes down to it, I feel like I follow a higher law."

Lazarus nodded. "I get that—that's why I'm willing to work with you right now. A more permanent alliance would necessitate you changing, though. I might be a product of the times but those are the times we're living in. I do think you're wrong if you believe I don't understand the necessity of taking harsh actions—I've done them in the past and will again. Still, we have to maintain a certain veneer of civilization." He reached up and touched his temple as a strange sensation washed over him—it was something familiar but he couldn't place it. He felt energized, though, as if he were suddenly flush with adrenaline.

"Hush," The Black Terror hissed, shocking Lazarus out of his reverie. When Lazarus and Lilith stopped and looked at him, he pointed with the cutlass down a narrow alleyway. "I just heard something," he whispered. "And I felt it in the ground, too…like something heavy was being moved over there."

All three of them felt it this time—a tremendous thump, followed quickly by another and then several more in succession.

Lilith drew her blade. "Not being moved," she said with a shake of her head. "Something big is *walking*."

After Lazarus drew his Magnum, the trio moved down the alleyway. Lazarus reached the end of the passage first, peering around the corner, his gaze starting at the ground and then moving upward. The Quietus—or at least what Lazarus assumed was the mysterious beast—was on the other side, his back to the hero. The creature was nearly fifteen feet in height with massive feet that were the size of anvils. Each time The Quietus took a step, the ground shook a bit and cracks appeared in the cobblestones. The heavy feet were attached to long, spindly legs that were a ghostly white in color, matching the rest of the body. Its buttocks jiggled loosely with each step and the bones of its spine jutted out against the flesh of its back. From the shoulders came long, muscular arms with hands that matched the feet in breadth. When its head turned slightly, Lazarus got a good look at it in profile—a bony, skull-like face that was, like the rest of it, completely hairless. Its nostrils were set flat against its face and the eyes were glowing orbs of yellow amidst stygian blackness. Its mouth was closed but the thin lips were parted slightly, revealing an overbite.

That sensation of feeling empowered filled Lazarus again, stronger than before. It seemed that proximity to The Quietus was the key to whatever this was.

The Black Terror hefted up his cutlass and hissed, "Now's my chance, while his back is to us."

Lazarus nodded and stepped aside, allowing his black-garbed ally to sprint past. The Black Terror gained momentum with each super-powered pump of his legs—unfortunately, the cobblestones were not conducive to sneaking up on anyone. The Quietus whirled about, eyes flashing, and it swung an oversized fist in a backhanded blow that caught Bob in the side of his body. The Black Terror went flying through the air, vanishing amidst plaster and dust as he broke through the exterior of a nearby building.

Lazarus was in motion as soon as he saw The Quietus spinning about—he sprang from the alley, moving several feet closer before dropping into a crouch. Bringing the Magnum up, he held it steady with both hands, aiming for the creature's right eye. He pulled the trigger and his shot flew straight and true—but at the last moment his foe threw up one of his oversized hands and the bullet lodged in its bone-white palm.

The Quietus bellowed in range, its voice sounding impossibly deep. With its other hand, it scratched at its wound, digging out the bullet and letting it fall to the ground. "Lazarus Gray...and Lilith?" The Quietus asked. "I had no idea the two of you knew one another."

Lilith moved forward as Lazarus stood, keeping his gun pointed at the massive figure that towered over them both. "You know us?"

"I live on the cusp of life and death...of course I know of you both," The Quietus replied, its thin lips pulling back into a rictus grin. "The woman that never dies...and the man that keeps coming back." He spread his hands out wide, blood oozing from his injured hand. He made no move to cover his nakedness and his genitals swayed with his every step. "I assume you've come here to try and kill me so that things will return to 'normal'?"

"Yes," Lazarus admitted, a flush coming over his cheeks. A strange "power" was growing within him and he suddenly remembered when he had last felt it—during the battle he'd had with Walther Lunt in the presence of Baba Yaga. She had insisted that if Lazarus wanted to return to life, he had to battle his oldest foe for the right to do so. He'd won, been fully restored to normality, and that strange sense of energy had faded almost immediately. Shaking his head, he asked, "I don't suppose you'd be willing to give up your power so that we could avoid a fight with you?"

The Quietus looked over as The Black Terror scrambled out of the wreckage, holding his sword in one hand. His leather uniform was filthy now and his cape was tattered but it was the expression of pure rage on his face that made the embodiment of living death let out a rumbling laugh. "No, Lazarus Gray, I shall not surrender my newfound power." He pointed a bony finger at The Black Terror. "Your sword was charged by Baba Yaga, wasn't it? I recognize her stench on you!"

Bob glared at Lazarus and asked, "Why are you two just standing there? Why aren't you attacking him?"

Lilith nodded, spinning her weapon through the air. "I agree, Lazarus—why aren't we?" Before the leader of Assistance Unlimited could respond, the eternal woman stabbed at her foe's nearest leg, the blade sinking deep into the meat. She gave it a twist, eliciting a scream of more rage than pain and then yanked her weapon from him —just in time for The Quietus to bring an oversized fist down upon her. The blow would have crushed her skull like an eggshell if Lazarus hadn't shoved her aside, leaving the attack to glance off her shoulder. Even so, Lilith gritted her teeth to stifle a cry—the entire side of her body suddenly flared with pain before going numb.

The Black Terror let out a roar, kicking off from the ground with his powerful leg muscles. He landed on the creature's shoulder and hefted his cutlass over his head with both hands before slamming it down into The Quietus' neck. Ichor spurted out over Bob's gloves and he had to hold on with all his might as his foe began to thrash about in an attempt to dislodge him.

While Lilith lay on the ground, trying to find her feet once more, and Bob held on for dear life, Lazarus found himself standing right in front of the colossal beast. He could sense invisible tendrils of energy swirling around The Quietus and he recognized the power of Un-Life, the delicate power that separated the living from the dead and sometimes caused one to become the other. He had once sacrificed himself to save the world, falling down into Hell to defeat a powerful foe. His trek back to the world of the living had been a difficult one and there had been an awful period where he had been not quite alive…but not dead either. The same energy that permeated the air around The Quietus had clung to Lazarus during that time and he'd never truly forgotten it. It had slipped past his waking consciousness, true, but now that he was confronted with it once more, he knew it and he *owned* it.

Lazarus tossed aside his pistol, instead spreading his hands out and taking several steps towards The Quietus. He lowered his head slightly, looking up through his lids at his foe. Raising his voice, he shouted, "Bob—don't let up! Lilith—I need you to distract him!"

Lilith let out a grunt as she found her footing. She held her weapon in her good hand, cradling her paralyzed other limb against her body. She moved forward as best she could, stabbing The Quietus in his dangling testicles. The monster roared in agony and Lazarus smiled coldly…he was no mage but he had a connection to this awful power and he had the necessary willpower to manipulate it. He hadn't expected that but now that it was right in front of him, he knew it was true. With every stab that both Lilith and The Black Terror produced, The Quietus was weakened…and Lazarus began pulling the power right out of him. It was not something that could be seen by the visible eye but it was happening nonetheless. Bit by bit, the power was slowly squeezed from The Quietus.

"No!" The Quietus bellowed. "It's not possible! You're just a human! Just a human!"

Lazarus shook his head. "There's no such thing as 'just a human.'" Lazarus clenched his hands into fists and The Quietus screamed, his eyes starting to dim and his legs giving way beneath him. As the big creature toppled over, Lilith rolled out of the way while The Black Terror pulled his sword free and jumped to safety. Lazarus remained where he was, seemingly daring the monster to land atop him. The Quietus landed just shy of him, the impact so close that the hair on Lazarus' head was ruffled.

The Black Terror moved closer to the twitching beast but his attention was entirely fixed on Lazarus. His mentor and teammate was crackling with power that raced up and down his limbs like tiny bursts of lightning. "Laz…?"

"I'm fine," Lazarus replied through gritted teeth. "I'm holding the power within me—you can kill him now. Just make it fast…I can't keep this up."

"No," The Quietus begged. "We can bargain…immortality for you and your loved ones. I can grant that!"

"I already have that," Lilith pointed out, still hobbling from her wounded side. "Immortality isn't all it's cracked up to be."

The Black Terror used a foot to shove The Quietus in the shoulder, rolling the massive beast onto his back. Clambering up on his chest, Bob stared down into the glowing eyes and sneered, "Don't look so frightened—you'll just regenerate eventually, won't you?"

"My spirit will roam the afterlife until I do," The Quietus replied. "You have no idea of the torments they save for me when I'm there!"

With a shrug, Bob raised his sword. He drove it down with all his might, stabbing it right where a human's heart would be. Apparently the anatomy of The Quietus was similar enough for a spout of blood erupted from the wound and the master of Un-Life gasped before his body gave a mighty shake and an exhalation of air from his lungs drove Bob back several steps. The fumes were noxious and made the hero cough.

Lazarus moaned, the power now so great within him that he seemed to glow with an internal light. Lilith could see his veins clearly and she knew that he was close to literally erupting. "Lazarus! Let it go!"

Dropping to his knees, Lazarus threw his head back and did just that—a bright burst of energy, so powerful that both Lilith and The Black Terror were forced to avert their eyes, shot forth from his eyes and mouth. It illuminated the night sky for many miles, the energy vanishing into the ether. It traveled 'round the world, stealing the second life from the walking corpses in Sovereign. The dead fell over wherever they stood, separated from their spirits once more.

When her vision cleared, Lilith saw that Lazarus was leaning forward and breathing heavily. With an effort, she knelt beside him and put her functioning arm around his shoulders. "Are you all right…?"

Lazarus let out a sharp burst of laughter and looked up into her eyes. He was covered in sweat and his eyes looked slightly mad but he sounded like himself as he responded, "I'll live."

The Black Terror was the first to notice that The Quietus was gone—

its entire bulk had vanished as soon as the energy had exploded outward from Lazarus. His sword remained, though it no longer glowed with the energy given it by Baba Yaga. Now that its work was done, the blade was back to its normal form. Picking it up, Bob sheathed it and asked, "How are we going to get home from here?"

Lazarus stood up, helping Lilith do the same. "I have a feeling that Abby will be here eventually. In the meantime, I think we should rest up."

Lilith smiled wanly. "Here, here."

CHAPTER XVIII
A BITTER POISON

PROFESSOR LIONEL THORNE stretched out across the soft sheets, relishing the comforts of freedom once more. He had been capable of freeing himself from Tartarus, of course, but the opportunity provided by his new friend Woland was too good to pass up. The sorcerer had lived up to his reputation, walking them right out of the prison. It had been Thorne's idea to go to one of his old safehouses and he'd whipped up a batch of his love potion before flopping onto his bed.

Once Woland had Lilith wrapped around his little finger, the two men would launch a campaign of vengeance that would bring Lazarus Gray to his knees. In fact, Thorne already had several ideas of what they could—

"You're insane."

The Professor sat up straight, frowning. Woland was standing there, holding the vial that Thorne had given him. The potion was within, a brownish color, tiny bubbles floating on the surface. "What are you talking about?" he asked.

"This!" Woland shouted, holding up the potion. "You said that this was what you bound Abby Cross with? That she was yours until you were forced to give up the antidote…"

"Yes. I told you all that."

"This is carbonated soda."

Thorne chuckled. "Oh, my friend...I know that chemistry is not your strong suit but trust me—that will work wonders for your former paramour."

Woland tossed it to the floor, sending the sticky, sweet fluid splashing. "Do you think me a fool?" he bellowed. "I should have known...you're insane. You only thought you ensnared her mind. The stories of you being a genius might have been true once but that was before you lost what intelligence you possessed!"

"See here now, I don't take well to insults!" Thorne stood up and walked around the spreading mess on the floor. He pointed a finger in Woland's face and warned, "Say something like that again and I'll teach you how to speak to your betters!"

"Betters!" Woland exclaimed with wide eyes. "Pompous fool..." He seized hold of Thorne's outstretched finger and twisted, which drew an outraged gasp from the other man...a gasp that quickly grew into a screech as Woland began to flood Thorne with heat. It started as a warm sensation traveling down the madman's arm but it quickly grew in intensity until Thorne felt as if his entire limb was encased in an oven. The skin began to peel away from the bone and his nerves exploded in pain. "You got my hopes up," Woland hissed, "and I despise that worse than anything else you could have done."

Releasing his hold on the other man, Woland tossed Thorne to the floor, where the man gave several powerful shudders before falling completely still. In truth, he had done nothing more than project the idea of severe pain into Thorne's mind, allowing the fellow's own growing fear to induce a heart attack.

Woland appreciated that Thorne had landed in the sticky mess that his madness had created...but it did nothing to ease the disappointment he felt. He had actually hoped that he could force Lilith to love him but he should have known that it would never have worked.

With a sigh, Woland exited the room and gathered up the few things he had acquired since leaving Tartarus. When he closed the door to Thorne's home behind him, he felt as if he were truly shutting a door to something much larger.

He walked down to a nearby pharmacy and used a pay phone to summon a taxi which arrived in due time.

Sliding into the backseat, he stared out the window as the cabbie twisted around and asked, "Where to, mac?"

"Tartarus."

The cabbie blinked. "You talkin' about that weird place on the outskirts of town? The land that belongs to Laz Gray and his pals?"

"That's the one."

"Whatcha goin' there for?"

"I shall be calling it home for the time being."

"You *live* there?" the cabbie asked, astonishment writ large on his features.

Without looking at the man, Woland gave a small shrug and answered, "There is no other place for me to call home…and I have lost the will to wander from place to place. So, again, I wish for you to take me to Tartarus. If you wish me to pay extra for the trouble of going to such an infamous locale, I am willing to do so."

With a shrug, the driver turned back around and shifted the car into drive. "Whatever you say, pal."

Woland was glad to be free of conversation for the rest of the trip. He would walk right up to the front door and turn himself back over for custody. Lilith had rejected him and he had lost hope of being able to win her back via schemes or treachery.

Perhaps, he mused, it had really come to the point in his life when he had to turn the page—she was gone, a part of his past, and he simply had to continue on until the End Times…and then he would finally know peace and, possibly, redemption.

For that last part, he would have to really change. No more plans of world subjugation. No more dealing with the forces of Hell. He had briefly come into contact with the Thirty Pieces of Silver and he'd felt their holy power. Even with all that had been done with them over the years, there was still a glow of Christ about them and Woland had been reminded of all that had been lost.

"It's never too late for forgiveness," he whispered to himself—and for the first time in a very long time, he meant it.

———◦◦◦◦◦———

LAZARUS AND ABBY exited Mayor Quinn's office, having explained to him that the crisis was over. City crews had been busy all over the city, lifting up the dead and beginning the time-consuming process of trying to return the corpses to their proper resting places. In many cases, Lazarus knew that the bodies would have to be moved to new homes since many old abandoned family cemeteries were unknown to officials. Local religious leaders were holding all sorts of vigils for their parishioners, many of whom had obvious spiritual concerns over recent events.

Lazarus slipped behind the wheel of his car, Abby taking a seat beside him. He glanced at her and asked, "What's wrong?"

She had been unusually quiet ever since their return to Sovereign and he'd tried to give her time to open up on her own but there was a limit to his patience. With a sigh, she replied, "A couple of things. First: I had that vision of Nakam being shot down by those silver bullets. That never happened—does that mean it might still take place? Second: I told you that Morgan refused to tell us all that happened when he was under the Grendel Tree. I'm convinced that whatever he saw or was told, it's eating away at him."

"I noticed he seemed more distracted than usual," Lazarus said as he started up the car and pulled out onto the busy city streets. "I assume it was something very personal...he saw his sister, correct?"

"Yes. That's what he says, anyway."

"So we give him a little more time before we press him on it."

The corner of Abby's mouth tilted upwards. "You give *him* time...

but you just come out and ask *me*?"

"Different people, different situation."

Abby nodded, accepting the answer. "And what about Nakam?"

"I was thinking about that…and I'm not certain that all your visions are meant to be taken literally. What you saw was Alf being struck down and you knew that it was by the silver bullets—but what if he were stuck down in another way besides the physical? And what if the silver bullets were merely the conduit for putting him in front of this 'attack'?"

"I'm still not following you," Abby admitted.

"You didn't notice the way he and that zeppelin captain were looking at each other this morning?" Lazarus didn't bother adding that it was Kelly that had pointed it out to him.

Abby blinked. "You think he was shot down…by love?" She let out a quick laugh, covering her mouth with one hand. "That's funny. A secret Jewish vigilante falling in love with an African airship commander… romance is a funny thing, isn't it?"

"I would agree with that," Lazarus replied. "Case in point: The Puzzler will be picked up by the local authorities this afternoon. His cousin has convinced him to turn himself in and do whatever's necessary to start over with a clean slate. Given that he's wanted for several murders, I'm not certain how well that will work out but I admire the attempt. If he could be rehabilitated, his intellect could be a wonderful weapon against crime."

"Bob's not going to believe that," Abby said, shaking her head.

Lazarus pulled into the underground garage located beneath their headquarters and parked into the stall reserved for his car. "Bob's been wrong before. We all have."

"True enough." Abby reached out and squeezed her mentor's hand, surprising him. "You led us through another difficult adventure, Lazarus. I don't know what any of us would do without you."

Lazarus turned to her, his mismatched eyes—one green, one

brown—staring into hers. "I'm not sure what I'd do without all of you," he admitted. "Hopefully neither of us will have to find out the answer to that anytime soon."

⊷∾⊶

MORGAN SLIPPED OUT of his room just past midnight, having waited until all of 6196 Robeson Avenue was silent. He wore blue silk pajamas embroidered with his initials on the pocket and slippers—all the better to ensure that he made as little noise as possible as he stole into his friend's private study. He made sure to close the door gently and didn't bother turning on the desk lamp until he was sure that no one had heard him enter.

The room was lined with bookshelves containing tomes on every topic imaginable. Morgan had been in the room so many times that he'd long ago stopped paying attention to the details...but now he peered intently at every shelf, looking for something that might indicate a hidden door. He hoped to find nothing...but he knew that he would. That was his sister he had talked to beneath the Grendel Tree and she had told him this.

He spotted it on his second look-through of the shelves: an oversized copy of the Bible bound in leather, jutting just a bit farther off the shelf than it should have. Reaching out with a trembling hand, Morgan gave the book a pull...and the entire wall suddenly swung inward, revealing a darkened room beyond. He could see nothing of what lay inside but he heard the sounds of bubbling water, making him think of aquarium fish tanks.

He pushed on into the gloom, the false wall swinging shut behind him. Reaching out with his hands, he felt along the walls until he found a light switch. When he activated it, his heart seemed to jump up from his chest into his throat...he'd thought many times about what he might find in this room but never in his wildest imaginings had he envisioned anything like this.

The room was roughly equal in size to the team's briefing room, with a metallic table in the center and several rolling chairs situated around it. Atop the table were a number of books, writing instruments, and a small tray containing the silver bullets that had caused so much trouble as of late.

It was the things that lined the room that were most shocking. There were eight large canisters, connected by a variety of tubes and pipes to the wall. Within each canister was a bubbling fluid that wasn't quite water, being a bit too thick for that, and within the fluid were bodies. They were all naked, eyes tightly closed as if in slumber, and breathing masks covered their noses and mouths. The one closest to him was shockingly familiar and Morgan moved to stand open-mouthed in front of it, his eyes moving up and down the female form within.

Shaking his head as if to clear it, he moved on to the next...and then to the next...his confusion and horror mounting with each recognizable face that he gazed upon.

It made no sense but the fact that Lazarus had hidden all of this, like some mad scientist, made him certain that the truth had to be something sinister.

It was when he looked in the last tank that his heart truly broke. He saw his own face mirrored back at him, identical to the one he saw every morning when he shaved...but sans the most recent scars and bruises that he'd picked up while in Africa.

Glancing back at the other tubes, he saw the others, all looking pristine and new...Samantha, Abby, Eun, Kelly, even Lazarus himself. For a moment, Morgan wondered why there wasn't a duplicate of Bob floating in one of the tanks but then he reasoned that perhaps the man's plant/human hybrid nature played a part.

The door to the room swung open and Morgan whirled about in alarm. His hand dropped to the pocket of his pajamas, where his pistol hung heavily. He paused when he saw it was Lazarus—even with all the questions racing through his mind, he wasn't prepared to draw a weapon on his friend.

Not yet.

Lazarus didn't seem surprised to find Morgan. Instead, he merely looked tired, as if he was preparing himself for an argument he'd had too many times before. "Good evening, Morgan," he said, closing the door behind him. "There's a sensor located next to the door," he said, gesturing towards a small penny-sized device located on the wall near the ceiling. "It lets me know if someone comes in here."

Without preamble, Morgan asked, "What the hell is all this...?"

Walking over to the metal table, Lazarus picked up a few loose papers and began organizing them into a small stack. "Are you aware that we share casefiles with some others in the city? Doc Daye, Gravedigger's crew..." Morgan shook his head and Lazarus continued. "A few years ago Gravedigger uncovered something strange going on at Drake Island[12]. I won't bore you with all the details but someone was making copies of people—he called them clones but they were also called 'ghosts' by some. Using a series of brilliant techniques, this man was able to grow new bodies of people from whom he had taken certain skin and blood samples. Their personalities and memories were held intact, stored in their DNA. The one drawback was that each of these entities only had the memories up to the time of their cloning—they wouldn't be aware of anything that had occurred after that first sample was taken. In order to get around that, you would need to have samples taken on a regular basis so that if the original died, you'd have a new clone emerge that would have memories as close to the time of death as possible. Knowledge of their clone status was shown to have a detrimental effect on the patients so it was advisable to keep that from them and let them believe they were the original."

Morgan stared at him for a moment, letting it all sink in. "Doctor Hancock's physicals...he's always taking blood samples."

Lazarus looked at him. "Yes."

"Because you want to have copies of us around in case we die."

"Not just you—me, too. It's a safeguard for all of us."

"And if I croaked, you'd just dump this...copy of me...out of the tank and nobody would be the wiser?" Morgan shook his head. "That's just sick. You know it wouldn't work, right? That thing couldn't pass for

---

12 This references the events of The Adventures of Gravedigger Volume 3.

me. Somebody would figure it out."

Lazarus said nothing, merely staring at him with a grave expression.

Morgan's shoulders began to slump and he asked, "You've already done it, haven't you? Who died...?"

"All of you, at one time or another."

"No," Morgan whispered, turning away from his friend. The implications were staggering and he knew he had to tell the others, let them know. Even if Lazarus had the best of intentions, this was too much...he should have told them, asked them if they wanted this. Even his own wife...!

"I know how you're feeling, Morgan...but after I came back from Hell, I knew that I had to take precautions. We all rely on each other and losing even one member of our family would be too much."

"You're not God, Lazarus," Morgan replied, rubbing his chin. He looked towards the door, planning to move towards it. "And if you think I'm going to stay silent on this, you're even crazier than I thought."

"It's not the first time."

Morgan turned quickly. "What do you mean?"

"It's not the first time you've figured it out...it's not always you, though. Last time it was Samantha. About six months ago."

Morgan's heart skipped a beat. "Please tell me you didn't--"

"I protected all of you. I protected us. I know it seems awful, Morgan, but you have to trust me."

"Or what? You'll kill me and replace me with another version of me?" Morgan shoved his hand into his pocket and seized hold of his pistol. What happened next was as fast as it was brutal—Lazarus spun about, launching a kick that caught Morgan on the side of his chin and snapped his neck in one clean hit.

Lazarus stood there for a moment after it was done, feeling a mixture of shame and relief. His lies would remain unknown and he felt certain that, at the core of it all, he was doing the right thing. When he had "died", the rest of the team had taken dangerous risks to bring him back...and earlier today Abby had voiced the secret truth that bound them all together: what would they do without each other? Lazarus knew what would happen...their carefully crafted world would fall apart and they'd all drift back to the way they'd been before they'd come together.

He knelt beside Morgan's corpse and touched it gently. "Sleep well, Morgan. You'll be back soon."

**TO BE CONTINUED IN
THE ADVENTURES OF LAZARUS GRAY VOLUME 12:
THE LIFE AND DEATH AND LIFE OF LAZARUS GRAY**

THE REESE UNLIMITED TIMELINE

THE REESE UNLIMITED TIMELINE

Major Events specific to certain stories and novels are included in brackets. Some of this information contains SPOILERS for The Peregrine, Lazarus Gray, Gravedigger and other stories.

~ 800 – Viking warrior Grimarr dies of disease but is resurrected as the Sword of Hel. He adventures for some time as Hel's agent on Earth. **[The Sword of Hel]**.

~ 1620 – Gwydion fab Dôn is captured by the witch Rhianna in France. She punishes him by binding his spirit to a bundle of rags. **["Gwydion," The Adventures of the Straw-Man Volume One]**

1748 – Johann Adam Weishaupt is born.

1750 – Guan-Yin embarks on a quest to find her lost father, which takes her to Skull Island **[Guan-Yin and the Horrors of Skull Island]**.

1774 – On June 23, 1774, General Benjamin Grove led the British forces through the air en route to Sovereign. What he did not know was that several local militia groups lay in wait for him. The resulting battle had been ferocious and deadly for both sides — in the end, only two men were left, one representing each side of the conflict: General Grove himself and a local youth by the name of Emmett Hain. **["The Choice," The Adventures of the Straw-Man Volume One]**

1776 – Johann Adam Weishaupt forms The Illuminati. He adopts the guise of the original Lazarus Gray in group meetings, reflecting his "rebirth" and the "moral ambiguity" of the group. In Sovereign City, a Hessian soldier dies in battle, his spirit resurrected as a headless warrior.

1782 – The man that would eventually be known as Gideon Black is born. **[The Second Book of Babylon]**

1793 – Mortimer Quinn comes to Sovereign City, investigating the tales of a Headless Horseman **[Gravedigger Volume One]**

1802 – Gideon Black's son is born and the chain of events that leads to Gideon being bonded with a suit of armor forged in Hell begins. Gideon is transformed into Babylon, a force for cosmic retribution. **[The Second Book of Babylon]**

1835 – Lucy Hale goes to work at Mendicott Hall. She meets Byron Mendicott and Lilith. **[The Chronicles of Lilith]**

1865 – Eobard Grace returns home from his actions in the American Civil War. Takes possession of the Book of Shadows from his uncle Frederick. **["The World of Shadow," The Family Grace: An Extraordinary History]**

1877 – Eobard Grace is summoned to the World of Shadows, where he battles Uris-Kor and fathers a son, Korben. **["The World of Shadow," The Family Grace: An Extraordinary History]**

1885 – Along with his niece Miriam and her paramour Ian Sinclair, Eobard returns to the World of Shadows to halt the merging of that world with Earth. **["The Flesh Wheel," The Family Grace: An Extraordinary History]**

1890 – Eobard fathers a second son, Leopold.

1893 – Eobard Grace successfully steals the Thirty Pieces of Silver that was paid to Judas for his betrayal of Jesus from The Illuminati. He melts the coins down into mystically-empowered silver and helps a friend forge these into bullets. They remain hidden in Atlanta, Georgia until the Forties. **[The Adventures of Lazarus Gray Volume 11]**

1895 – Felix Cole (The Bookbinder) is born.

1900 – Max Davies is born to publisher Warren Davies and his wife, heiress Margaret Davies.

1901 – Leonid Kaslov is born.

1905 – Richard Winthrop is born in San Francisco.

1908 – Warren Davies is murdered by Ted Grossett, a killer nicknamed

"Death's Head". **["Lucifer's Cage", the Peregrine Volume One**, more details shown in **"Origins," the Peregrine Volume One]** Hans Merkel kills his own father. **["Blitzkrieg," the Peregrine Volume One]**. Abigail Cross is born in Tennessee.

1910 – Evelyn Gould is born.

1912 – Byron Mendicott travels to France to kill Lucy Hale. **[The Chronicles of Lilith]**

1913 – Felix Cole meets the Cockroach Man and becomes part of The Great Work. **["The Great Work," The Family Grace: An Extraordinary History]** Bart Hill is born in Sovereign City [Revealed in **The Adventures of Lazarus Gray Volume 14]**

1914 – Margaret Davies passes away in her sleep. Max is adopted by his uncle Reginald.

1915 – Felix Cole marries Charlotte Grace, Eobard Grace's cousin.

1916 – Leonid Kaslov's father Nikolai becomes involved in the plot to assassinate Rasputin.

1917 – Betsy Cole is born to Felix and Charlotte Grace Cole. Nikolai Kaslov is murdered.

1918 – Max Davies begins wandering the world. Richard Winthrop's parents die in an accident.

1922 – Warlike Manchu tutors Max Davies in Kyoto.

1925 – Max Davies becomes the Peregrine, operating throughout Europe.

1926 – Charlotte Grace dies. Richard Winthrop has a brief romance with exchange student Sarah Dumas.

1927 – Richard Winthrop graduates from Yale. On the night of his graduation, he is recruited into The Illuminati. Max and Leopold Grace battle the Red Lord in Paris. Richard Winthrop meets Miya Shimada in Japan, where he purchases The McGuinness Obelisk for The Illuminati. Bart Hill begins adventuring as a teenaged Daredevil.

1928 – The Peregrine returns to Boston. Dexter van Melkebeek [later to be known as The Darkling] receives his training in Tibet from Tenzin. Sheridan Masters loses his fiance Carmen in a terrible mystic storm in Egypt. He is trapped in Carcosa for several years.

1929 – Max Davies is one of the judges for the Miss Beantown contest [**"The Miss Beantown Affair," The Peregrine Volume Three**]. Richard Winthrop destroys a coven of vampires in Mexico.

1930 – Richard Winthrop pursues The Devil's Heart in Peru [**"Eidolon," Lazarus Gray Volume Three**].

1932 – The Peregrine hunts down his father's killer [**"Origins," the Peregrine Volume One**]. The Darkling returns to the United States.

1933 – Jacob Trench uncovers Lucifer's Cage. [**"Lucifer's Cage", the Peregrine Volume One**] The Peregrine battles Doctor York [**All-Star Pulp Comics # 1**] After a failed attempt at betraying The Illuminati, Richard Winthrop wakes up on the shores of Sovereign City with no memory of his name or past. He has only one clue to his past in his possession: a small medallion adorned with the words Lazarus Gray and the image of a naked man with the head of a lion. [**"The Girl With the Phantom Eyes," Lazarus Gray Volume One**]. The man who would eventually call himself Paul Alfred Müller-Murnau arrives in Sovereign on the same night as Lazarus Gray. [**"Nemesis, "Lazarus Gray Volume Six**].

1934 – Now calling himself Lazarus Gray, Richard Winthrop forms Assistance Unlimited in Sovereign City. He recruits Samantha Grace, Morgan Watts and Eun Jiwon [**"The Girl With the Phantom Eyes," Lazarus Gray Volume One**] Walther Lunt aids German scientists in unleashing the power of Die Glocke, which in turn frees the demonic forces of Satan's Circus [**"Die Glocke," Lazarus Gray Volume Two**]. The entity who will become known as The Black Terror is created [**"The Making of a Hero," Lazarus Gray Volume Two**].

1935 – Felix Cole and his daughter Betsy seek out the Book of Eibon. **["The Great Work," The Family Grace: An Extraordinary History]** Assistance Unlimited undertakes a number of missions, defeating the likes of Walther Lunt, Doc Pemberley, Malcolm Goodwill & Black Heart, Princess Femi & The Undying, Mr. Skull, The Axeman and The Yellow Claw **["The Girl With the Phantom Eyes," "The Devil's Bible," "The Corpse Screams at Midnight," "The Burning Skull," "The Axeman of Sovereign City,"** and **"The God of Hate," Lazarus Gray Volume One]** The Peregrine journeys to Sovereign City and teams up with Assistance Unlimited to battle Devil Face. They also encounter a new hero – The Dark Gentleman. **["Darkness, Spreading Its Wings of Black," The Peregrine Volume Two** and **Lazarus Gray Volume One].** Lazarus Gray and Assistance Unlimited become embroiled in the search for Die Glocke **["Die Glocke," Lazarus Gray Volume Two]**

1936 – Assistance Unlimited completes their hunt for Die Glocke and confronts the threat of Jack-In-Irons. Abigail Cross and Jakob Sporrenberg join Assistance Unlimited **["Die Glocke," Lazarus Gray Volume Two].** The Peregrine moves to Atlanta and recovers the Dagger of Elohim from Felix Darkholme. The Peregrine meets Evelyn Gould. The Peregrine battles Jacob Trench. **["Lucifer's Cage", the Peregrine Volume One].** Reed Barrows revives Camilla. **["Kingdom of Blood," The Peregrine Volume One].** Kevin Atwill is abandoned in the Amazonian jungle by his friends, a victim of the Gorgon legacy. **["The Gorgon Conspiracy," The Peregrine Volume One].** Nathaniel Caine's lover is killed by Tweedledum while Dan Daring looks on **["Catalyst," The Peregrine Volume One]** Assistance Unlimited teams up with The Black Terror to battle Prometheus and The Titan in South America **["The Making of a Hero," Lazarus Gray Volume Two].** Doc Pemberley allies himself with Abraham Klee, Stanley Davis and Constance Majestros to form Murder Unlimited. Lazarus Gray is able to defeat this confederation of evil and Pemberley finds himself the victim of Doctor Satan's machinations **["Murder Unlimited," Lazarus Gray Volume Three].** Lazarus Gray is forced to compete with The Darkling for possession of a set of demonic bones. During the course of this, a member of Assistance Unlimited becomes Eidolon. **["Eidolon," Lazarus Gray Volume Three].** Charity Grace dies and is reborn as the first female Gravedigger. **[Gravedigger Volume One].** Dr. York attempts to revive Princess Femi so that she can aid him in battling The Peregrine ["**The Peregrine Animated Script**," **The Peregrine Volume Three**]. The Dark Gentleman confronts The Shadow Court and brings them to justice. ["**The Judgment of the Shadow Court**," **The Adventures of The Dark Gentleman Book One**]. A few weeks later, The Dark Gentleman learns the truth about Amadeus Crouch ["**The Silver Room**," **The Adventures of The Dark Gentleman Book Two**].

1937 – Max and Evelyn marry. Camilla attempts to create the Kingdom of Blood. World's ancient vampires awaken and the Peregrine is 'marked' by Nyarlathotep. Gerhard Klempt's experiments are halted. William McKenzie becomes Chief of Police in Atlanta. The Peregrine meets Benson, who clears his record with the police. ["**Kingdom of Blood**," **the Peregrine Volume One**]. Lazarus Gray and Assistance Unlimited teams up with Thunder Jim Wade to confront the deadly threat of Leviathan ["**Leviathan Rising**", **Lazarus Gray Volume Four**]. Hank Wilbon is murdered, leading to his eventual resurrection as the Reaper. ["**Kaslov's Fire**, "**The Peregrine Volume One**]. The Peregrine and Evelyn become unwelcome guests of Baron Werner Prescott, eventually foiling his attempts to create an artificial island and a weather-controlling weapon for the Nazis ["**The Killing Games,** " **The Peregrine Volume Three**] Gravedigger confronts a series of terrible threats in Sovereign City, including Thanatos, a gender-swapping satanic cult and The Headless Horseman. Charity and Samantha Grace make peace about their status as half-sisters. [**Gravedigger Volume One**] Lazarus Gray teams with Eidolon and The Darkling to combat Doctor Satan ["**Satan's Circus**," **Lazarus Gray Volume Four**]. Lazarus Gray battles the forces of Wilson Brisk and Skyrider. The Three Sisters are unleashed upon Sovereign City ["**The Felonious Financier**," **Lazarus Gray Volume Five**]. Gravedigger confronts the twin threats of Hiroshi Tamaki and the immortal known as Pandora [**Gravedigger Volume Two**]. Lazarus Gray travels to Cape Noire to investigate the mysterious vigilante known as Brother Bones ["**Shadows and Phantoms**, "**Lazarus Gray Volume Five**]. The villain known as The Basilisk attempts to seize control of Sovereign City's underworld ["**Stare of The Basilisk**," **Lazarus Gray Volume Five**]. The Three Sisters unite with Princess Femi to combat Assistance Unlimited. Sobek's attempt to destroy Femi helps lead young Madison Montgomery into a role as Femi's handmaiden. Lazarus gets engaged to Kelly Emerson ["**Immortals**," **Lazarus Gray Volume**

Five]. Lazarus and Kelly are married. ["Wedding Bells," Lazarus Gray Volume Five]

1938 – The Peregrine travels to Great City to aid the Moon Man in battling Lycos and his Gasping Death. The Peregrine destroys the physical shell of Nyarlathotep and gains his trademark signet ring. ["The Gasping Death," The Peregrine Volume One]. The jungle hero known as the Revenant is killed ["Death from the Jungle," The Peregrine Volume Two]. Gravedigger, Lazarus Gray and The Peregrine come together to confront the terrible events known as Götterdämmerung. Many other heroes – including The Black Bat, The Black Terror, The Darkling and Leonid Kaslov are caught up in the events, as well. The insane villain Mr. Death is created. [Götterdämmerung]. Three months after Götterdämmerung, Assistance Unlimited battles The Librarian and adds The Black Terror to the team. ["The Affair of the Familiar Corpse," Lazarus Gray Volume Six]. Assistance Unlimited journeys to Europe where they reunite with Eidolon and Abby. The group then teams up with a Berlin-based hero known as Nakam to battle Mr. Death and The Torch. Lazarus Gray confronts the spirit of Walther Lunt and Baba Yaga. ["The Strands of Fate," Lazarus Gray Volume Six]. Mortimer Quinn is elected mayor of Sovereign City. Paul Alfred Müller-Murnau learns of his role as Nemesis and becomes an ally of Princess Femi and Madison Montgomery. Femi gains possession of the fabled Emerald Tablet. Abby becomes warden of Tartarus. ["Nemesis," Lazarus Gray Volume Six]. Assistance Unlimited battles an out-of-control Golem and an agent of the OFP codenamed Heidi Von Sinn. Kelly's pregnancy takes an odd turn after exposure to an Aryan idol. ["Tapestry," Lazarus Gray Volume Six]. Daniel Higgins bonds with the Hell-forged armor and becomes Babylon. His sister Stella is killed. [The Second Book of Babylon]

1939 – Ibis and the Warlike Manchu revive the Abomination. Evelyn becomes pregnant and gives birth to their first child, a boy named William. ["Abominations," The Peregrine Volume One]. The Peregrine allies himself with Leonid Kaslov to stop the Reaper's attacks and to foil the plans of Rasputin. ["Kaslov's Fire," the Peregrine Volume One] Violet Cambridge and Will McKenzie become embroiled in the hunt for a mystical item known as The Damned Thing [The Damned Thing] Assistance Unlimited teams up with Sheridan Masters to investigate a deadly alliance between Femi and a masked villain called El Demonio. The evils summon Hastur, the King In Yellow, and Lazarus is forced to travel to Carcosa. Kelly learns that their unborn child is infused with Vril energy. Femi and Madison Montgomery are both apparently destroyed. [Lazarus Gray Volume Seven]. Gravedigger engages in a war of wits with The King, a battle that leaves The Dark Gentleman dead and her forces in disarray. She uncovers the connection between The Voice and Nestorius – then stands for judgment before Anubis. [Gravedigger Volume Three]. Lazarus and Kelly Gray become the parents of Ezekiel Gray, Samantha Grace learns she's pregnant ["The Santa Slaying", Lazarus Gray Volume Eight].

1940 - Samantha discovers that Paul Alfred Müller-Murnau is responsible for her mystic pregnancy. Müller-Murnau forms a new version of Murder Unlimited alongside Bushido, Brick, Vixen and Alloy. ["As Above, So Below," Lazarus Gray Volume Eight]. The Warlike Manchu returns with a new pupil — Hans Merkel, aka Shinigami. The Warlike Manchu kidnaps William Davies but the Peregrine and Leonid Kaslov manage to rescue the boy. ["Blitzkrieg, "the Peregrine Volume One] The Peregrine journeys to Germany alongside the Domino Lady and Will McKenzie to combat the demonic organization known as Bloodwerks. ["Bloodwerks," the Peregrine Volume One] Lazarus Gray encounters Gravedigger and a heroine from another universe while in Istanbul. The trio end up battling an alliance between Princess Femi and a villain from another world. A loosely-affiliated grouping of female heroes consisting of Lady Peregrine [Evelyn Davies], Jet Girl, Fantomah and Kitten is formed. [Worlds Apart]. Samantha Grace gives birth to her daughter Emily. Assistance Unlimited battle a werewolf and free a young woman whose dreams are incredibly powerful ["The Girl That Dreamed, "Lazarus Gray Volume Eight]. Kevin Atwill seeks revenge against his former friends, bringing him into conflict with the Peregrine ["The Gorgon Conspiracy," The Peregrine Volume One]. The Peregrine takes a young vampire under his care, protecting him from a cult that worships a race of beings known as The Shambling Ones. With the aid of Leonid Kazlov, the cult is destroyed /"The Shambling Ones," The Peregrine Volume One]. Daniel Higgins and his sister Stella stumble onto a mob killing and Stella is badly injured. Daniel finds a strange suit of armor and bonds with it, becoming transformed into Babylon [The Second Book of Babylon]. Lazarus Gray and Assistance

Unlimited travel to Kentucky to investigate the disappearance of a young girl. Eidolon quits the team after a debate about how to resolve the crisis ["It Wants To Kill You," Lazarus Gray Volume Eight]. Nemesis and Bushido join up with the Occult Forces Project to resurrect The Speaker from the Stars. They are opposed and ultimately foiled by Assistance Unlimited and The Golden Amazon ["The Speaker from the Stars," Lazarus Gray Volume Eight].

1941 – Philip Gallagher, a journalist, uncovers the Peregrine's secret identity but chooses to become an ally of the vigilante rather than reveal it to the world ["Origins," the Peregrine Volume One]. The Peregrine teams with the Black Bat and Ascott Keane, as well as a reluctant Doctor Satan, in defeating the plans of the sorcerer Arias ["The Bleeding Hells", The Peregrine Volume One]. The Peregrine rescues McKenzie from the Iron Maiden ["The Iron Maiden," The Peregrine Volume One]. Asgard falls and Thor's hammer ends up in the hands of his daughter, whose spirit is hidden away in the body of a young woman on Earth. Loki and his assistant Durok end up working alongside Murder Unlimited [Nemesis, Bushido, The Golden Amazon and Eidolon] to try and flood the world so that it can remade along Loki's wishes. In the hidden world of Vorium, Assistance Unlimited teams with The Fighting Yank to foil their plans. The Golden Amazon and The Fighting Yank both become occasional members of Assistance Unlimited. Nemesis and Bushido are both killed. ["The Sinking World," Lazarus Gray Volume Nine]. In November, The Golden Amazon, The Fighting Yank and The Black Terror journey to Manhattan to team with Olga Mesmer to stop a plot by Doctor Satan and his consort [Lady Satan]. The foursome remain together as The Heroes, an offshoot organization of Assistance Unlimited. The Black Terror agrees to serve as a liaison between the teams. ["Satan's Lair", Lazarus Gray Volume Ten]. Tommy McDuff is injured during the attack on Pearl Harbor – he is taken from the military hospital by Eris, the Goddess of Discord. She gave him great power but at the cost of his sanity – as Phasma, he embarked on a scheme to use 'The Torch of Ç'thalpa to tear down many of the institutions of power. He worked with Rosemary Lunt [the daughter of Walther Lunt] and was opposed by Assistance Unlimited and Babylon. The villainous Billhook releases damaging information about Assistance Unlimited to the press. Lazarus Gray agrees to work with Major Caruso and Project: Cicada. [Lazarus Gray Volume Ten].

1942 – The Peregrine battles a Nazi super agent known as the Grim Reaper, who is attempting to gather the Crystal Skulls ["**The Three Skulls," The Peregrine Volume One**]. The Peregrine becomes embroiled in a plot by Sun Koh and a group of Axis killers known as The Furies. The Peregrine and Sun Koh end up in a deadly battle on the banks of the Potomac River. ["**The Scorched God," The Peregrine Volume Two**]. In London, the Peregrine and Evelyn meet Nathaniel Caine [aka the Catalyst] and Rachel Winters, who are involved in stopping the Nazis from creating the Un Earth. They battle Doctor Satan and the Black Zeppelin ["**Catalyst," The Peregrine Volume One**]. Evelyn learns she's pregnant with a second child. The Peregrine solves the mystery of the Roanoke Colony ["**The Lost Colony," The Peregrine Volume One**]. The Peregrine battles against an arsonist in the employ of Bennecio Tommasso ["**Where There's Smoke", The Peregrine Volume Three**]. The Warlike Manchu is revived and embarks upon a search for the Philosopher's Stone ["**The Resurrection Gambit," The Peregrine Volume One**]. Joseph Williams is born [son of Mitchell and Charity]. Assistance Unlimited is forced to work with Nakam and Lilith [leader of the Crimson Ladies] to stop a plot formulated by a mystic named Woland and The Black Terror's archenemy, The Puzzler. The dead are raised in Sovereign City but Lazarus and his allies are able to eventually turn the tide with an assist from The Revenant and Baba Yaga. In the end, a shocking revelation is made that alters Morgan Watts' life forever. [**The Adventures of Lazarus Gray Volume Eleven**].

1943 – The Peregrine teams with Xander to deal with the Onyx Raven ["**The Onyx Raven", The Peregrine Volume Three**]. The Peregrine is confronted by the twin threats of Fernando Pasarin and the undead pirate Hendrik van der Decken ["**The Phantom Vessel," The Peregrine Volume Two**]. Evelyn and Max become the parents of a second child, Emma Davies. The Peregrine teams with the daughter of the Revenant to battle Hermann Krupp and the Golden Goblin ["**Death from the Jungle," The Peregrine Volume Two**] The Peregrine battles Doctor Satan over possession of an ancient Mayan tablet ["**The Four Peregrines," The Peregrine Volume Two**]. The Peregrine travels to Peru to battle an undead magician called The Spook ["**Spook," The Peregrine Volume Two**]. The Peregrine clashes with Doctor Death, who briefly takes possession of Will McKenzie ["**The Peregrine**

Nevermore," The Peregrine Volume Three]. Baron Rudolph Gustav gains possession of the Rod of Aaron and kidnaps Evelyn, forcing the Peregrine into an uneasy alliance with the Warlike Manchu ["Dead of Night," The Peregrine Volume Two]. Doctor Satan flees to the hidden land of Vorium, where the Peregrine allies with Frankenstein's Monster to bring him to justice ["Satan's Trial," The Peregrine Volume Two]. Tim Roland is recruited by The Flame and Miss Masque ["The Ivory Machine," The Peregrine Volume Two]. The Black Terror investigates a German attempt to replicate his powers and becomes friends with a scientist named Clarke ["Terrors", The Peregrine Volume Two]. Assistance Unlimited and The Heroes come together to work with L'Homme Fantastique in returning Lazarus Gray to normalcy. El Demonio and a return visit to Carcosa are involved [Lazarus Gray Volume 12]. Rama-Memnon, Teddy Pumpkins, and Rose Dorcas lay waste to Sovereign City but are defeated by the combined forces of Assistance Unlimited, Nature Boy, Eidolon and Wynona Jones. Jakob Sporrenberg transitions from Eidolon to being The Observer. [Lazarus Gray Volume 13].

1944 – The Peregrine organizes a strike force composed of Revenant, Frankenstein's Monster, Catalyst and Esper. The group is known as The Claws of the Peregrine and they take part in two notable adventures in this year: against the diabolical Mr. Dee and then later against an alliance between Doctor Satan and the Warlike Manchu ["The Diabolical Mr. Dee" and "A Plague of Wicked Men", The Peregrine Volume Two]. Daredevil [Bart Hill] is recruited to join Assistance Unlimited [Lazarus Gray Volume 14]

1946 – The Peregrine discovers that Adolph Hitler is still alive and has become a vampire in service to Dracula. In an attempt to stop the villains from using the Holy Lance to take over the world, the Peregrine allies with the Claws of the Peregrine, a time traveler named Jenny Everywhere, a thief called Belladonna and Leonid Kaslov. The villains are defeated and Max's future is revealed to still be in doubt. Events shown from 2006 on are just a possible future. The Peregrine also has several encounters with a demonically powered killer known as Stickman. ["The Devil's Spear," The Peregrine Omnibus Volume Two]. The Peregrine encounters a madman named Samuel Garibaldi [aka Rainman] and his ally, Dr. Gottlieb Hochmuller. The Peregrine and his Claws team defeat the villainous duo and several new heroes join the ranks of the Claws team — Miss Masque, Black Terror & Tim and The Flame. [**"The Ivory Machine," The Peregrine Volume Two**]

1947 – The Peregrine and Lady Peregrine do battle with Dr. York once more, as the madman attempts to revive the elder gods. [**"The Murder Mansion," The Peregrine Volume 7**]

1948 – SIGIL [Supreme International Group for Illegal Liaisons] is formed out of the remnants of the Nazis and The Illuminati. [**Assistance Unlimited: The Silver Age – Broken Empire**]

1953 – The Peregrine acquires the Looking Glass from Lu Chang. [**"Black Mass," The Peregrine Volume One**]

1961 – Max's son William becomes the second Peregrine. [**"The Four Peregrines," The Peregrine Volume Two**]

1964 – Mitchell Williams passes away from cancer. Charity Grace is invited to join Assistance Unlimited by her niece, Emily. [**Gravedigger Volume Three**]. Benjamin Falk, a former Secret Service Agent, is recruited into Assistance Unlimited. Alongside Emily Grace, Sato Shinji, Ezekiel Gray and Bart Hill, he assists in defeating an attempted Fourth Reich led by Marvin Levin and his clone army. Emily and Ezekiel then lead a battle with the forces of SIGIL [Supreme International Group for Illegal Liaisons] and a would-be god named Helios. [**Assistance Unlimited: The Silver Age – Broken Empire**]

1967 – The second Peregrine battles and defeats the Warlike Manchu, who is in possession of the Mayan Tablet that Doctor Satan coveted in '43. Evelyn Davies dies. [**"The Four Peregrines," The Peregrine Volume Two**]

1970 – William Davies [the second Peregrine] commits suicide by jumping from a Manhattan rooftop. Emma Davies [Max's daughter and William's sister] becomes the Peregrine one week later, in February. [**"The Four Peregrines, " The Peregrine Volume Two**]

1973 – The third Peregrine is accompanied by Kayla Kaslov [daughter